Short, Long and Tall Stories

Stuart Kear

Stuart Kear

Copyright © 2017 Stuart Kear

All rights reserved.

ISBN:1981208534
ISBN-13:9781981208531

DEDICATION

To the memory of my much loved wife of 48 years, Bunty, for her goading and believing in me and my family for their support

CONTENTS

	Acknowledgments	i
1	Duty	1
2	The Accident	9
3	The Bedroom	17
4	The Dig at the Station Hotel	21
5	The Letter	40
6	The Look	43
7	The Messenger	50
8	The Departure	60
9	The Learning Game	65
10	The Vicar's Wife	71
11	The Incident at the Belgrave Hotel	79
12	Christmas Crackers	87
13	The Message on the Wall	91

Stuart Kear

DUTY

Travelling back to Wales was a nightmare. The weather was atrocious, the traffic heavy. Conditions were not ideal for some in-depth thought, which was disappointing as I needed to try and sort myself out. I was at a cross road in my life. I wanted to gather all the facts, run them by my emotions, and decide in which direction the rest of my life lay. Driving was normally the method I employed when needing to make a major decision. Generally I enjoyed the process, not today however. Not only were driving conditions bad, there were several facets in my life to which I was not able to bring experience to bear, and yet they seemed to me to be inextricably linked.

The news that I was to be a father at the age of 38 had come as a considerable shock. I had not lived the life of a monk sharing my life with a few girls, but the relationships had not lasted more than a few weeks being curtailed usually by me. Sandra was different. I had to admit that things were more comfortable with her. She had moved in after only three weeks and I felt none of the previous constraints, but a permanent relationship I had not really thought about. We had not discussed the future together. Now a baby completely out of the blue, leaving me extremely confused. The nearest to babies I had been were the smaller brothers or sisters of the pupils I taught at the Comprehensive. Did I want all this responsibility, was I capable of handling such a situation.

A blast from the extremely loud horn of an articulated lorry, cascading spray from its many wheels, brought me back to the situation at hand. I drove concentrating on the road. Turning off the M5 Motorway and onto the M50, the traffic eased as I passed into Wales and the reason I was on this journey.

I had not seen my father for twelve years. That had been at my mother's funeral, when I had driven down and back the same day. I had not spoken to either of my parents, or tried to contact them since I left home for University when I was eighteen. The situation seemed mutually agreeable as nothing came from their direction either. The news of his death came officially by letter from his solicitor. This legal eagle held the keys to the house and would administer the will. As an only child matters should move smoothly and quickly I was assured, but the family effects and contents of the house needed attention. Apparently only I could decide on this course of action.

The emotional triangle seemed intact. I was to help administer the conclusion of the life of a man I felt nothing for, and yet who was my father, consider whether I could spend the rest of my time on earth with a person I really hardly knew, or share that time, and be responsible for a life that had barely started to form. It was an experience that I had already started badly. Sandra had told me about the baby only last night and I had left early this morning, leaving only a note to say I would ring when I arrived at my father's house. I was regretting that already.

I was surprised to find that there were now several Hotels close to my father's home that I could use. In my time at home Hotels were only in Cardiff, or one or two scattered in larger townships. I had chosen one only a few miles away from my destination and reserved a room. I could not bring myself to believe no matter how objectively I thought about it, that I could sleep overnight in the house.

As I approached my native area, the rain had cleared, clouds hanging on the mountain tops being chased away by the sun. I was amazed. At the time of my leaving Coal, Heavy Industry and Commerce had been masters of the environment, and the black scars of their triumph were everywhere, and in plain view. Now the reverse appeared to be the case, the countryside had recovered, colour had replaced black. Trees covered the hillsides as they must have done centuries before, with hardly a blemish to mar the views. Green was now predominant in all of its many shades. New roads by-passed villages gave new perspectives on the Valley, which gave me the feeling that I was seeing the place for the first time. The metamorphosis that had taken place was stunning to eyes that remembered smokey, grey bleakness in a forgotten landscape. It was a pleasure to see what can be achieved from the most unlikely scenarios.

I drew in to the street where my family's house stood. The houses had been described rather superciliously as Villas in those far off days, socially very desirable at that time. Looked at today they are terraced houses with bay windows, a small postage stamp garden as a forecourt. Still pleasant enough homes but, those wishing to aspire housing wise now look to the three or four bedroom detached with its own garage.

Pulling up outside the house, number twenty two, I was aware of another sea change in the large numbers of cars parked in the street. Where did children play now I wondered, as I closed the car door? Resting my forearms on the roof the car, I looked up at the house that had been a cold and remote home to me through my early life.

Five steps up to a red brick arched doorway. The dark green front door with two frosted glass panels was inset, creating a porch. The brass knocker, letter box and numbers, still shone dully. To the right of the doorway was the bay window. Above, the two flat bedroom windows, all painted in the same depressing hue as the door, all views to the inside protected by the ubiquitous net curtains. My father had paved our forecourt many years ago, avoiding the necessity to be seen at the front tending a garden however small. The front of the house had not changed in nearly forty years, and it sent a chill up my spine.

As I was musing the front door opened. My heart skipping a beat I took a step backwards as I fully expected my father to come out, but it was the Solicitor who thanked me for being punctual, handed me the keys, said he would see me tomorrow as planned, and drove away. I entered the house I had left so many years ago.

Closing the front door, I stood in the hallway hesitant to enter further, to open myself to a past that I had worked steadfastly to close, far behind me. The hurt buried deep inside, had been thickly layered over the years of living here. At ages when understanding rejection is not possible, only bewilderment and self- doubt exist, and if it

remains unexplained and uncared for, it corrodes the bonds that bind people and families together. The reflections were however pointless, I was here now a grown man, and it would be a test of my maturity to face those memories of this house, hopefully with the objectivity that time can sometimes bring.

I walked through the house. There had been changes, things wear out. Modern science had provided labour saving devices and comforts of which even my father had seen the benefits. A television stared blankly from the corner. Blazing arguments had taken place trying to achieve one of those, all of which I had lost, and now here it stood. Many items of furniture still remained, and prodded my memory banks, the kitchen table where many a cold and silent meal had taken place, with a child not knowing why. Upstairs nothing appeared to have changed. My parents separate bedrooms still remained. My Father's just as he had left it, apart from his best suit, which I understood from the solicitor he was to be buried in. I'd smiled ruefully when I read that. Old habits die hard, "waste not want not", I could still hear him saying it. My old bedroom was much like my Mother's, empty, which was not a surprise, apart from a framed graduation photograph of me, which was. That must have been erected in a moment of weakness. I believe that the final twelve years of my Father's life to have been his happiest. He had lived alone, and was able to follow his lifetime regimes, of thrift and insularity, without any deviations. The male version of a Black Widow spider.

His personal effects were in the bureau that doubled as a desk. One of my lasting images had been of him sitting at this desk half turned in the chair, face twisted under Horn rimmed glasses, hair Brylcreamed back, thin lips spitting vitriol, complaining to my Mother of the expense of one thing or another.

Trawling through the contents of the desk was a pointless, exercise. Mr. Roberts the efficient Solicitor had all the necessary papers. I abandoned it. Save for an old leather wallet that caught my eye. It contained just three Black and White photographs yellowing with age. I glanced at and discarded them they were of people I could not know. Yet something, there was something. Picking up the top photograph it showed four young men, obviously on a camping holiday. They stood together smiling happily, dressed in long shorts and white vests.

I stared closer at the man on one end. Could it be? The hair was darker but the style was the same. He was of about the same size and shape, it was the slightly crossed front teeth that did it, this was my father.

My father in a vest and shorts, the image was quite unbelievable to me. I had never seen him other than fully dressed at any time. Laughing was similarly foreign. If I tried really hard, the possible memory of a smile perhaps, but laughing never, the longer I looked the greater the gap between the image and the man I knew. A question began to form in my mind, what could have made such a difference, how could an obviously happy young man, with at least three friends, turn into a friendless unhappy adult.

The telephone rang, the sudden noise made me jump. I had been lost in the past. Picking up the receiver, a warm familiar voice said,

"Hello, is that you David?" Sandra's tone was hesitant,

"Yes it's me, I was just about to ring you", I lied, cursing myself for not doing so.

"I bet", she laughed good naturedly, "The weather was so bad I just wondered if you'd arrived all right ?", her concern made me feel even worse "You'd left so early, you should have woken me," She said nothing about yesterday's bombshell. "Listen I know you have much to do, I just wanted to make sure you were all right, ring me when you can, O.K.".

"O.K.", I said inadequately, and Sandra was gone.

I suppose at some point in my life someone else must have cared this much about me, but if they had I could not remember who it was. Sandra was like a warm drink on a cold night, and I wanted to hold that warmth in my hands and keep it close.

However the change in my father's character gripped me. I wanted to find out what had altered him. The only person I could think of was Aunty Jo. She wasn't an aunt by blood, just a friend of my Mother's. She was also the only person that had shown me any kind of affection through those early years. The close family atmosphere in the house so accentuated the difference to my own, and I spent as much time there as I was allowed, little as it was. I found the house, not surprising myself that I could. It was a minute or two before recognition dawned in the eyes of the stout, bespectacled old lady.

"David is it really you? I'd so hoped you'd come" she cried, opening her arms in welcome.

It was an hour or so and several cups of tea, before I could broach the subject I had come to question her about. Eventually I brought out the photographs, and gently offered the subject of my parents, in particular my father.

"This is a very sad story David", the old lady began "It's a story of how pride and being unforgiving can ruin lives. Your parents were engaged to be married and very happy about it they were. However your father was very keen on cycling, and he and his friends often went away on weekends". She pointed to the photographs, to indicate that this was one of them.

"About three or four months before the Wedding they decided on one last jaunt", she continued, "but one of his friends could not go for some reason I never knew. Coincidentally the travelling fair was in the valley, your Mother and some of us girls decided to go as the boys were away. Sort of a Hen party you know, we became quite brazen, and had a few drinks. Your Mother not being used it got quite tiddley, we lost her in the crowd. We didn't worry they were all locals, and the night passed." She stopped for another cup of tea.

"Look David", she began again obviously wanting to unburden herself, "To cut this story short, and I'm sorry if this comes as a shock, your Mother became pregnant with you before the Wedding, and to save her reputation she did not tell your father until later. There now that's the truth of it, your father was not your real father." She sat back hands folded across her ample stomach, chins wobbling.

I didn't know whether she expected me to collapse in a heap or what, but it somehow came as no surprise and I felt little.

"What happened after she told him?" I asked somewhat meekly.

"Your Mother only told me of this many years later you understand, and I was sworn to secrecy. I have never told another living soul." she admitted nobly, "Your father being a very proud man told her that if she revealed the name of the man involved, he would stay with her and bring you up as his own. But she wouldn't or couldn't. His suspicions fell on the friend missing on the cycling trip, though nothing was ever proved."

"Yet he stayed with us", I stated

"But at what cost?" asked Aunty Jo philosophically "He didn't leave because he didn't want everyone to know, his pride would not allow it. But he could not forgive either. In fact as the years past he hardened his heart against your Mother, everything and everybody, and the sight of you each day only served to remind him of the slight to his manhood. It eventually drove you away and killed your Mother. He had been wronged, but his sense of duty as he saw it tore you all apart".

She was right. I felt immeasurably lighter, her explanations had released a subconscious rucksack of self-imposed guilt. I now felt some sympathy and a little understanding for my mother but it was way too late, too much time had passed, the situation had been no fault of mine. The light of truth also exposed the complete waste of their two lives, and the stunting effect upon my own.

In that instant I realised that I loved Sandra, and the baby would strengthen our bond not destroy it. It would be cherished and shown love, hopefully growing into a complete person.

There was nothing to keep me here, no more time to waste, and only one place I wanted to be. I stood, asking Aunty Jo if I could use her telephone.

Sandra's welcoming voice made me ache.

"Hi, it's me," I said softly "I'm coming home".

Stuart Kear

THE ACCIDENT

He looked down at the young man's back. Saw the as yet immature muscles softly rippling under the fair skin as he worked down on his knees, stripped to the waist hewing at the narrow seam of coal. He noticed too the fine blond hair running the length of the workingman's spine. It had collected coal dust abundant in the air, and his sweat had created narrow channels as it ran down his back.

He was surprised at the acuteness of his vision in the limited light of the lantern, and he momentarily observed the differences in their physique. The younger working man was taller, slimmer and fair of hair. Whilst he, the observer, was of shorter, thick-set build, typical mining stock with thick black wiry hair. His other senses were also heightened too. The sound of the tools hitting the coal reverberated in his ears. His touch was clammy yet sensitive. The adrenaline coursed through his body as his brain anticipated his impending actions.

They had been working together until a few minutes before. When under the pretext of being thirsty he had gone for a drink of water. This had not actually been a lie. His mouth was dry. But his main intention was to be in the correct position when his signal came.

He stood behind and slightly to the workingman's left. His stealthy movements covered by the gentle singing of the other as he worked. He stood there, temples pounding. The actions he was about to take would achieve the main objective of his plan, namely the death of the man before him. He was about to kill him. No going back.

He grasped his chosen weapon, a heavy working shovel with a curved blade. The normality of the tool was crucial in his plan for a strange implement found later might jeopardize the whole plot.

He had based his plan and the timing for the act upon an explosion made by shot blasting, loosening stubborn deposits of coal further into the workings of the mine. The blasting was inevitably punctual. Everyone had to know when and where it was going to happen.

He and his partner were working just far enough away from the area to be considered safe. Safe is a relative word working in low tunnels a mile beneath the earth's surface. Unpredictability was the only thing to depend on. He was, he knew, taking an extreme calculated risk in carrying out his dangerous actions, but if successful it would be foolproof.

The plan had been devised quite coldly and logically over some weeks, after waking one morning and realising that he was quite simply determined to commit the act of murder. The act would banish and expunge from his life all possibilities of further humiliation, frustration, jealousy and emotional turmoil caused by the other man.

Upon hearing the shrill whistled warning, and the muffled boom of the controlled explosion his body vibrated, sweat flowed freely from him. He grasped the smooth wooden handle of the shovel firmly, forced himself to breathe deeply once, twice, he then raised the weapon behind him and swung it down in a flat scything arc. Down with all his pent-up emotions, the amalgam of hatred, bunched in his biceps and shoulders driving the curved edge of the shovel blade directly at the workingman's neck, just at the base of his skull.

But in those previous seconds, probably as a result of vibrations caused by the explosion, three stones fell from the partially unsupported roof of the tunnel. One the size of a dinner plate fell harmlessly to the young miner's right. Another smaller stone fell behind him, but the third stone about the size of a walnut fell onto the crown of his helmet. It caused the most natural of human reflexes. The man looked up. Not out of injury or pain, merely satisfying a basic self-protecting instinct of curiosity. Where had the stone come from and were there more to follow?

That simple reaction now acted as double security, for upon looking up the physical movement of his head re-positioned his helmet further down and covered his neck.

The assassin saw all this happening before him. As his weapon flashed towards its target, everything appeared to slow down into a dream-like state. He saw the stone fall and hit the helmet, he knew what the response would be. The man's head raised and the helmet tilted down protectively, and yet he was powerless to stop the swing of his arms.

He was rudely brought back to reality by the shuddering impact of metal on metal. His aim has been true, but instead of yielding flesh and bone receiving the blow here was hard metal cushioning the skull. The result was tremendous. The shock of the impact sent tremors up the shaft of the shovel up through his hands, arms and ultimately his brain. He shuddered under the after-shock. The action had been literally stunning, but not as he had planned, mortal. His victim lay prone on the floor of the tunnel at his feet.

Sweat dripped from his eyebrows, nose and chin, and his breathing came in short gasps as his body reacted to the emotional tempest of what he had done. He bent over the still figure to confirm its pulse was still beating. He glanced furtively at the badly damaged helmet. It had done its protective work.

He had to finish the gruesome task he had started. Using the largest of the stones that had fallen earlier he executed an unplanned secondary strike. Then he could loosen and cause more stone to fall from the roof of the tunnel. His actions would be covered. His mind raced down the pathways of his plan, the now enforced small detour of another blow incidental.

The deliberate creation of a small roof fall had been the main strand of his alibi strategy. If he could make the roof fall look genuine then the assumption would be that a tragic accident had occurred. The death would be recorded just as another statistic. it happened all too often in the mining industry. It was feasible, he had the skills to make it so, and if he could he would be free forever.

He forced his thoughts through his now focused brain as he realised the stakes in his premeditated gamble were at their highest. He now had a race against time. Men would be returning to clear away, and to load into drams the coal blasted free further into the workings. He had to be somewhere else, anywhere, before that occurred.
He stood astride the legs of the still motionless figure beneath him. Removing the nearest roof support beam, he worked at the roof with an iron bar. He prayed that something large enough might fall and save him the gory task of the terminal strike.

The sound of a low rumble made him stop. He cocked his head to one side listening intently, like a rabbit hearing the on-coming traffic and trying to ascertain its direction. At first he thought it was empty drams being brought up to be filled. The sixth sense born of years' of underground work made him realise that the sound, like distant thunder, had come from above, his whole being screamed at him to run. This was the point of evolution giving you a tenuous sense for self-preservation.

However, his hatred and his determination to end the existence of the man at his feet, held him fast. He told his natural instincts that its message was awry and there was yet time to finish his task.

He was wrong. He should have obeyed that primeval call.

As he reached over the body, the tunnel along its whole length collapsed about him in a roaring, terrifying, crashing boom. Rocks flattened over him and pinned him to the body of his victim. In that last excruciating moment before his life was forced from him, he thought that if only he had waited one more day, fate and the forces of nature would have achieved his savage desire for him.

The rescue parties took some ten hours to reach their bodies, as rock, shale, coal and earth was cleared away carefully. Roof supports vigilantly replaced for fear of further falls, the rescuers moved inexorably forward, until a tattered and bloody trouser leg appeared from the rubble. All other work ceased.

All hands now concentrated on carefully removing and clearing the immediate vicinity of the find. Slowly, everything was hand-picked away, and the bodies were exposed. They lay one on top of the other. Legs and arms twisted into unnatural shapes. The topmost body, back broken, was covered in coal-saturated blood.

The rescuers stood in a silent circle around the grisly tableau that lay before them. In the dust-laden air, turned yellow by the lights from their lanterns, they heaved and panted from the pace of their efforts, and looked down on this demoralising spectacle.

The First Aid man was quickly on the scene, examining the bodies for signs of life. He sadly shook his head as he searched for a pulse on the larger upper body. Then he drew an excited short breath as his fingers located the faintest of beats on the lower body's bloodied neck.

"Carefully now boys" he said gently" The young one's barely alive, but alive he is, let's get them out and away from this Hell-Hole. Perhaps your work and that man's brave actions will not have been in vain, this terrible day".

"What actions do you mean" asked one miner, his eyes shining white in his coal-dust blackened face.

"Why surely you can see what happened here" replied the medical-man sharply. "The older man realised there was no escape for them, and so threw himself over the youngster in an attempt to protect him, and I'm going to see that it was an act that will not go unrewarded".

The other miners murmured their approval of this version of events, and rejuvenated by their discovery of life, set their faces once more to the wall of rubble that confronted them. Their hopes rekindled belief that perhaps other lives might yet be saved.

The two bodies were put on stretchers and quickly borne away, onward and eventually upward into the light and fresh pure air.

The news of the discovery raced ahead of the stretcher party, passing excitedly along from explaining mouth to eagerly recipient ear, each version being embroidered upon the last. The unofficial version hammered on the front door of the anxious and grimly expectant family of the victims. It was immediately admitted.

As with families and carers the world over, in the aftermath of disasters large and small, the waiting is a dark moonscape of peaks and ridges of raised hopes, plateaus of past memories and abysses of blackest fears. The final news, good or bad, at least produces a shaft of reality, and the human mind's defence against madness, the emotions, are released.

The messenger stood respectfully before the Mother of the two men and imparted the news, twisting his cap in his hands, exposing his nervousness at his task.

"Your sons are found" he almost whispered " and one is alive" he raised his voice exultantly, as if bringing forward the good news would somehow lessen the impact and inevitable consequences of his statement. "But one was lost outright by the force of the roof fall". He started to move away, when the woman before him spoke, her voice strained and hesitant with emotion.

"Which one......?" Her voice trailed away unable to complete the inevitable question, but her eyes held his firmly.

The messenger stood his ground and answered "Your eldest son died protecting his younger brother with his own body". He looked deeply into her eyes expecting to see only grief and sadness, but he caught something quite unexpected. In that sober face he saw for the briefest of moments, jubilation and relief burn brightly, before returning to a sorrowful, downcast stare.

The morning of the memorial service was bright and cheerful; the service of remembrance had been preceded by a ceremony. The Mother of the two brothers had been presented with a medal commemorating her eldest son's actions. The Choir had sung, and the minister had been exhaustive in his plaudits. The congregation had begun to leave the Chapel, when two old friends greeted one another.

They had been neighbours of the mourning family, but one had moved away some months before the accident, and they had not seen each other since that time. They embraced warmly and both agreed that it had been a very moving service, and how marvellously the younger brother had sung.

"What a voice he has, and what a poignant figure he struck, still so pale and his arm in a sling. I think everyone cried" said the old neighbour.

"Yes he is the soloist with the Choir now and soon to go on to the college of music. He passed his examinations just before the accident," informed the other.

"That is excellent news indeed, but wasn't the elder brother a member of the Choir too ?" enquired the visitor.

"Not of late," his friend replied. "He certainly had been a member quite a good voice too, but he appeared to lose interest, and stopped attending Choir practices some months ago", then leaning forward, voice lowered in the best gossiping fashion he added "Did you notice the girl in the front seat gazing rapturously at our soloist this morning?. They are engaged to be married, planning to be married as soon as his college course is finished".

"Yes", admitted the visitor "you could not help but notice, and I thought I recognised her". Needing to confirm the suspicions building in his mind he enquired "But wasn't she walking out with the elder brother when we lived here"

"It all came to nothing", informed the conspirator "His Mother put a stop to it, telling him the girl was too young for him and not strong enough to be a miner's wife".

"Really" mused the other thoughtfully. "Still there could not have been any animosity between them could there ?". The question hung mildly in the air.

"Good Lord no" the question was dismissed immediately. "I think actions speak louder than words don't you. Greater Love Hath No Man Than To Lay Down His Life For His Brother, the Bible says doesn't it ?" the neighbour quoted irritably.

"Yes of course you are right" the friend said condescendingly, and they walked away in the pale sunshine together.

Stuart Kear

THE BEDROOM

She was feeling no pain now a little woozy perhaps but very tired, it was the morphine and she was grateful for it.

She was, by her own request, propped up high with pillows, she could have anything she wanted now. Her time was short, she knew it as did everyone else. The Doctor and the District Nurse were professionally calm and efficient, kind, caring without fuss. She appreciated that but it was different for family. They were trying to control their emotions, not quite knowing what to do or say. How are you today is somewhat superfluous when today might be the last day, as it will be very soon.

She had asked to be propped up because it was a sunny spring day and in the afternoon the Sun travelled around the house and beamed like a Golden Searchlight into the bedroom at the back of the terraced house. The Sunlight cast the shadow of the window frame onto the carpet and lapped up and onto the bottom of the bed illuminating the pinks and greens of the little flowers decorating the white candlewick bedspread. The whole of the room lit up, the light catching the picture frames, wardrobe and the chest of drawers handles glittered. She loved it.

She also loved it for the memories it engendered of the afternoons many, many years before when she and Harry would make love on the bed bathed in the sunlight. It had been warm and wonderful, wistfully bringing him back closer to her now when she needed him most.

Through the window she could see the mountain on the other side of the valley. The daffodils she and Harry had planted would be standing proudly now pronouncing through their custard yellow trumpets that spring had arrived, encouraging everyone to enjoy the passing of the grey barren days of winter and the change to a season of colour and new beginnings.

This was life endlessly moving on she thought, soon to leave her behind as it would ultimately for everyone.

This room symbolised life for her too, it was where her two children had been born and where she too had been born as a woman after her wedding to Harry and where she had learned about living and loving, where innocence turned to maturity.

It had been hard at times but she had been happy, she felt fulfilled. Her passing would mean the completion of her circle of life. She had loved and been loved in return and she was content with that.

After the funeral Diane the daughter and elder of the two children took on the onerous task of clearing the bedroom of her Mother's things.

She did this quite dispassionately for although she had loved her mother she had come to despise this room. Indeed she now hated the whole house for its smallness and the fact that it was part of a terrace. She hated being cheek by jowl with others constantly popping in knowing your whole life.

The house also represented her Mother's life of hard uncompromising toil. She had been from the generation of few labour saving devices, of coal fires, strikes and wars, when the woman's place was shackled to the home. The eagle eyes of neighbours kept her worrying about the whiteness of her window nets and the sheets upon her washing line every Monday, the observance of the expected way of doing things properly.

Diane knew it had held the family in good stead but it was not her way. She was not prepared for her life to be scrutinised, her clothes, relationships, opinions, her whole being, by other people. She was no-one else's business.

Glimpsing life over the rim of the valley's mountains Diane had liked what she had seen. Preferring the open fields of country life and now lived on an isolated farm away from all this living in a beehive. She wanted freedom of thought of movement and mobility. Time and life had moved on and she wanted more from it.

She would leave this bedroom and its symbolism never to return.

Derek the son, stood in his mother's bedroom, he and some friends had come to empty the rooms of the furniture ready to sell the house, his sister had insisted.

He stood and experienced the intensity of his mother's presence. He had spent many nights in his mother's bed as a child when his father worked the late shift. Her warmth and closeness had formed an unbreakable bond between them and he had been devastated with her passing. The bedroom resonated with her neatness and sense of order, something he had inherited from her.

He loved this house with its myriad happy memories so much so that he lived in one just like it. He liked valley living with its sense of community, camaraderie and caring with family and friends close to hand. It was how he had been happily brought up. His morals, his work ethic, his beliefs all had been bred into him or taught here at his parent's knees. It was an integral part of him. It was his inner core, who he was.

He did not understand his sister's eagerness to move on, to cut the ties that bind. On to what, some lonely outpost in the middle of the country constantly travelling, yet it seemed to him she was going nowhere, while his roots grew seemingly deeper with every passing year.

They were brother and sister born of the same parents, of the same blood, but they were completely different people. He recognised it but could not come to terms with it.

He looked around and thought that if he were to pass on as contentedly as his mother in a bedroom such as this one then that would be fine with him.

THE DIG AT THE STATION HOTEL

The Station Hotel was a" Dinosaur", a " Relic", a "Thing of the Past, Uneconomic in its Present Condition", a" Statement of the Valleys' Past", and "This After All, Was 1965". The words of the young Brewery Architect hung in the air like cobwebs long after he had gone and Griff Lewis kept walking into them, brushing them away, but they kept coming back to remind him of what was going to happen in the near future.

Redevelopment. The word had hit him straight between the eyes, for the word also meant retirement for him. That was not what bothered him, if the truth were told the place was getting a bit too much for him now anyway. A quick glance in a bar mirror showed him an ageing, bespectacled man with a paunch and thinning grey hair, re-enforcing his view.

Redevelopment into what, the thought sent a shiver up his spine, surely not one of the new-fangled Pubs with Flock wallpaper, low claustrophobic ceilings, and God forbid, frothy beer from electronic pumps. He sought solace by sitting in the bar after closing time one afternoon, and looked around.

The Station Hotel had been built in 1882 of dressed stone and real timbers. It had been built in the Valleys' boom years, the years of the Black Yukon, when men from all over the world came to the Valleys to work the coal, more men than there was housing for, and with the coming of the railways The Station Hotel and all the other Station Hotels had been built.

Within its impressive two storey facade were twenty rooms, and for better than Sixty years most of the rooms had been occupied by as large a mix of humanity as could be imagined. New incoming mine workers, travelling salesman, actors, boxers, con-men, all of the human flotsam and jetsam that supports, and lives off a boom town.

The two bars of the Station Hotel were either side of the double fronted doors. The bars faced onto the street, announcing their separate identities by advertising the fact in frosted glass. "Saloon Bar" and "Lounge Bar", written in large letters, and just in case of confusion, the two half glass doors also had the words emblazoned on them. The words decorated with swirls and fancy work were defended by diagonal brass push bars worn smooth and shiny by years of pushing and polish. Inside the bars were similar in size and shape, both having fine high ceilings, with cornice work, and decorated ceiling roses. From these ceilings ornamented gas lighting had once hung but that had now been acceptably replaced by electric bulbs in large opaque glass bowls. However the difference between the Saloon and Lounge bars, and the lifestyles associated with them was in the fittings.

In the Saloon Bar was a high shining hardwood topped and panelled bar running for most if it's length. Pump handles, standing like enamelled cricket stumps were strategically placed along it. A Brass foot-rail also ran the length of the bar
for the comfort of those who preferred to drink at the bar.

The floor was of flagstone, and the furnishings comprised of wooden chairs and tables, tables large enough for cards or dominoes, with four or more chairs, that scraped the flagstones noisily when moved. The emulsioned walls were decorated with plaques and cups of by-gone sports days and nights successes, essentially and enforceably men only in those days.

The Lounge Bar had a smaller, semi-circular bar in one corner, giving more room for tables and upholstered chairs. Ladies were allowed here, only accompanied by men in the early days, but times had changed. Changes had brought concessions to comfort such as carpet, curtains, wallpaper and some pictures, altogether a cosier atmosphere.

This was proper Pub. So thought Griff Lewis after living, and working here for most of his Sixty Two years, initially with his parents, and after his father died, with his mother, and subsequently his wife.

Wife...The word summed up an episode in his life, that still rankled, and the venom in the memory surprised him by raising his temperature, he suddenly felt hot. He had tried very hard to forget her. He had married her relatively late in life, she had been much younger than himself and had turned out to be "flighty", the old fashioned adjective his mother had used to describe her seemed too polite. Too polite to conjure up the faithless, scheming bitch he had known.

The anger rose in his throat again when he thought of the men, and of the money taken from the till, the humiliation he had suffered at her hand until the confrontation when the worn thread had finally snapped.

He had caught her with a Scottish soldier, out in the back yard, and had beaten the Scot to a pulp. Then turning on her he slapped her face knocking her to the ground. She had gone off with the soldier, and they were never heard of again in the valley. She had gone from him, and the door had closed on the only truly dark period of his life.

Griff looked at his hands, they quite damp with sweat. He thought a walk around the Pub would calm down his inner thoughts. He went upstairs to let the cool atmosphere and the spirits of the past inhabitants wash over him.

He entered the rooms above one by one, walked to the window in each room, and looked out at the same view, each time from a slightly different angle. He stood with his back to the small fireplaces as if warming himself, an attitude he was sure every one of the previous inhabitants had adopted at some time during their tenancy.

In one or two of the rooms things were slightly in disarray, where the architect and his minions had investigated, a raised floorboard here, some hacked off plasterwork there.

In number Fourteen, a slightly smaller room, overlooking the back yard and outhouses that once had been stables and storehouses, the small cast iron fire surround had been levered off the wall on one side, for what purpose he could not imagine, but it gave the impression that it was about to fall. Griff was a tidy man, not fastidious, but tidy he liked things to look right, and so with the heel of his hand, he attempted to bump the fire place back into position. It took three tries before it yielded and straightened. He stood back to assess his handy-work and as he did something dropped into the empty hearth.

He bent and picked it up. It was something wrapped in a piece of tarpaulin or similar material. Unwrapping it he found it was an old school exercise book, yellowed pages stuck together, faded writing stronger in places weaker in others.

He could not read the words, so stopped to put on his glasses. They did not make any difference he still could not read the writing. Suddenly he realized why. It was written in another language. Welsh was his instant thought and he looked closer. Although not able to speak Welsh, like many Valley people, he thought he would be able to recognise certain words. Nothing. He looked from faded cover to faded cover, he could recognise nothing.

His mind raced and excited questions flooded him. What tongue was it in Who had put it there ? Why hide it ? What to do ?. He looked at his watch, "Damn" he thought it was close to evening opening time. This would have to wait.

Griff leaned on the bar and looked toward the door. He could tell almost to the minute when his regular customers would arrive, and what they would drink. Some nights he would challenge himself to be pulling the correct drink for the respective customer as they walked into the bar.

Tonight was different.

He was waiting for two particular customers, his life long friends and bosom companions Tom Parry and Hugh Brian Williams. H.B. as was popularly known, both for his initials and also after his favourite expression "Hells Bells". He had an uncanny knack of bringing it along with a hundred different emphases into ever topic of conversation or discussion. Precisely at 7.30 p.m. they entered the bar and took up their usual positions.

Griff pulled their pints quickly, he quietly told them of the day's events.

H.B.'s bright blue eyes immediately sparkled under his thatch of salt and pepper hair that had once been red. His natural effervescence was always ready to pop given a new interest.

"Hells Bells" said H.B. predictably, this time in a long drawn out fashion. "There's a turn ujp, where's the book then" he asked almost bouncing up and down on the spot. "Let's have a look, perhaps we can spot something".

Tom Parry as ever spoke slowly and sagely. Tom, tall, dark , strong and dependable in any situation, typical mining stock.

"I don't see why H.B. we all went to the same school, and if Griff couldn't read it why should we"

Griff showed them the book anyway, urging them to hurry before more people started arriving, as he did not want the world to know.

"Well" said Tom the quicker of the two friends "If you want my opinion, its written in Spanish".

"Spanish ?" questioned Griff, "And what brings you to that conclusion Tom?".

"Because there is one word that I recognise", said Tom "Seville, that's a Spanish place. I remember because I saw it the other day when I unwrapped an Orange, and it was printed on that white tissue paper, they wrap them in".

"Hells Bells he's right you know", said H.B. quickly.

On this somewhat tenuous point they agreed, but that raised another, more pressing problem.

"Right, Spanish it is then. Now, who do we know that can speak Spanish ?" said Griff, and went off to serve other customers. He returned after a few minutes of stilted conversation with them. He was impatient to carry on their deductions. He found Tom and H.B. faces bright with inspiration.

"Bill Francis" said H.B obviously pleased with his contribution.

"Why Billy Francis," questioned Griff "I've never heard him speaking Spanish".

"Well Hells Bells Griff, don't you remember, he went to fight in the

Spanish Civil War in the International Brigade".

"Good God, that was over Thirty years ago, he'll never still speak it will he" posed Griff.

"Do you know anyone else in this Valley likely to speak it", asked Tom, negative looks all round. "Well he'll have to do then won't he". Down went the pint glasses and off they went to find Bill Francis to do his best.

An hour or so later they returned with a protesting Bill Francis in tow. Bill was a stocky, grizzled, goatee bearded man with glasses that rested half way down the bridge of his nose.

He was shown the book as surreptitiously as they could, in the now well populated bar. He confirmed that it was written in Spanish. Tom looked smug. However, Bill insisted that it would take some time for him to study and translate the book, as his Spanish was very rusty not having used it for quite some time.

Yes, yes the trio patronisingly agreed, and gave him a maximum of two days to come up with a preliminary report. He was sworn to secrecy, given the book, bought a pint and sent on his way, no sense in wasting any more time.

"Hells Bells this is bloody great isn't it ", said H.B. excitedly.

Bill Francis returned late the third evening, looking rather strained.

"I've done my best boys", he said, "I've had to put two and two together in some places where I could not understand the writing, but I think I've got the gist of it".

"Well", said Griff expectantly.

"Well," said Bill, "You might not want to hear what I've got to tell you, I think it better we wait until everyone else has gone home Griff". The trio looked at one another anxiously.

"Oh Hells Bells Bill, I can't wait", said H.B. nervously excited.

Wait he had to however, because Bill was not going to chance being interrupted in his telling of the tale after the effort he had put in to interpret it

The four settled into seats in Griff's sitting room, after the bar had been cleared somewhat unceremoniously, and bang on time much to the surprise of the many regulars, but Griff had complained of being depressed by the news of the future of the Pub. This was true, and understandable in the circumstances, and so the other customers had gone off mumbling good-naturedly into the night. Back to equally surprised wives at home not expecting their spouses for another half an hour or so.

"It appears Griff", began Bill, "That you or rather your Mother, once had a young Spanish boy for a lodger. He had left home at sixteen to go to sea, with all the romantic notions that boys' read about in books. The romance did not last long, he hated it, the crew on the freighter he was on used and abused him, he was beaten and half starved, he decided to jump ship, his chance came in Cardiff docks and he took it. He heard of a Spanish community in Merthyr Tydfil, working in the Iron Works, and walked the Twenty miles or so to Merthyr to find them. Bill stopped for a drink provided from the bar by Griff.

"Did he find them', asked Griff impatiently,

"Yes I'm coming to that" said the storyteller raising his eyes to the ceiling. "He found them all right. He arrived worn and weary, confused in a landscape he found completely hostile. Cold, wet valleys, clogged with people and industry, where-as he was used to the hot open plains of agricultural Spain. However his countrymen took him in, fed him, and found him a job in the iron works, and for a little while he settled. All too soon however things began to change, his countrymen albeit Spaniards, were rough city outcasts mainly from Seville, thieves and gamblers who had left Spain as much to escape the clutches of the law as anything else. He knew, being a country lad that he could not stay with them. Biding his time, picking up enough English to make himself understood and saving a little money, he left the group and come here to hew coal and earn enough money to return to Spain, where his heart he now realised still remained.

Bill drained his glass, Griff refilled his and all the other glasses and returned as quickly as he could, looking at the others as he did so he caught their look of rapt attention, awaiting the next segment of the unfolding story, as he himself was.

Bill began once more, "Your Mother must have taken him in Griff, and he found work easily enough at the pit, the Station Hotel must have suited him, because he says he feels happier and more settled now that at any other time since he had left his home, although he is still dead set on returning",

Yes my Mother's cooking helped, I suppose", ventured Griff.

"So far, so good" said Bill, sitting upright in his seat, and looking up from his text and surveying the men, like a teacher about to admonish his class. "Up to now that's just about an exact translation, word for word so to speak, but now the problems started, both for me and our boy. Just at this point the writing started to fade, and two or three pages in the old book were stuck together, and parting them, without damaging the print was impossible". He help up the excersize book for the men to see, and towards the middle he exposed three pages, with some small tears, and scrapes, where he had tried valiantly, but unsuccessfully to keep them whole.

"However", Bill continued, " picking out as many words as I could, reading on to keep pace with events, and then turning back to fill in I think my version of events is reasonably accurate".

"Fair enough Bill," said Tom, "We can see that you tried hard to keep it all intact, so we'll accept your version, as we wouldn't know any bloody different anyway would we ?".

"Quite right Tom," said Griff "Carry on Bill, you mentioned that the boy had some problems too".

"He certainly does", said Bill reverting to his previous position for reading, in the big armchair, "For something happens that changes all his plans", he paused for effect, "He met a girl", another pause,

Tom chipped in quickly with a wink "Oh yes, they normally do"

"Yes, but not like that this time", said Bill slightly huffily, he was the teacher again, whose tale had been halted by a smutty juvenile remark, Tom pursed his lips as Bill continued. "It appears that he met her late one night, returning home after working overtime on an afternoon shift. He had heard her crying in a shop doorway, she had been cast out from her home, some time before, and had wandered about until she had become very weak, distressed and was now quite ill. He recognises this and being a very compassionate lad, he says he understands what it is to be lonely and friendless, and he sees it as his duty to help her. He brings her back to his room, but knowing your Mother's rule about visitors particularly ladies staying overnight Griff, he is extremely careful. A few days go by, and with some warmth and a little food, some care and attention, she appears to respond, and gets a little stronger. However it is only temporary, she is basically too weak, and after just four days, she dies."

Bill stops for effect and looks up.

Anxious looks flash between the other three men, suddenly what had started out as almost a bedtime story, had taken a somewhat dramatic and uncertain twist. Bill pressed on unrelentingly.

"He's heartbroken, she was the only one to whom he has given his affection, in this God forsaken country, and now she has gone, and he has a real problem. He has a body on his hands.

Who can he confide in? Who can help him ? Desperation sets in. He cannot tell your Mother, Griff, because he knows that she would be bound to inform the police, who would immediately think that he had murdered the girl, and would lock him up or worse".

"Well Hells Bells, a post mortem will have told the police, how ill she was, and he would have been all right, " said H.B., who had been quieter this evening, than at any time since his appendix operation two years ago.

"Yes, we know that, but he's a bloody Spaniard, and young one at that, and so wasn't to know was he", said Griff, who was now completely engrossed, and wanted to know more, "Go on Bill, what did he do with her", he was sitting noticeably further forward in his seat, his face thrust out as if he wanted to look over the edge of Bill's book.

"Well, he knows that he has to get rid of her body, but where" Bill's voice takes on the tone of a conspirator. "After searching his racing mind, he realises that it must be very close to hand as he cannot carry a body far, and, after a quick look around, the only place he can think of is the stables".

"What, my stables," said Griff quietly but incredulously.

"Yes, your stables", said Bill pointedly "At that time your Mother did not have any animals in there, and so it can only have held bits and pieces, and was not visited a great deal. So that night he carried her down the back stairs, into the stable, and buried her there.

After that he stayed on for a week, to avoid looking as if he was running away, worked a week's notice, wrote this diary as a document of defence as he sees it, pays up and is off. He catches the first available boat back to the Sun, his family and Spain. That is as near an explanation of the facts as I can give you, gentlemen" finished Bill.

He put down the old excersize book, and his notes, sitting back in the armchair, with an air of satisfaction of one who has fulfilled a contract. There was a stillness in the air broken only by the sound of Adams Apples rising and falling, as drinks go down and questions come up.

"Now hold on just a minute Bill, let me get this clear: said Griff concernedly, "Are you telling me that I've got a young girl's body buried in my stables".

"Yes" said Bill turning to the relevant page, and pointing to the faded script. Here it is look, Esta Muerta, she's dead", he translated, turned the pages gingerly and pointed again," En La Cuadra, in the stables, it's quite clear".

"Hells Bells", said H.B. in a long exhaled fashion.

There followed some minutes of silence, as each man let his mind absorb the events of the story, eventually Tom Parry spoke. "Well that's as sad a story as I've heard in a long time", the other nodded in silent agreement. "To think that young girl has lain in your stable all this time Griff.

"Yes" said Griff in a distant thoughtful fashion.

"Doesn't seem right somehow that she should be out there", they turned to the speaker, who was Bill Francis.

"What do you mean Bill", asked Tom questioningly. "Well she had precious little out of life when she was here, and is getting even less now she is lying out there in unconsecrated ground, can't be right can it. To be comfortable in the hereafter, you have to be laid in a proper grave don't you", said Bill in a voice that made a statement rather than asked a question.

"Well she has been out there a long time now, I would think she must be used to being in whatever place and condition she's in", said Griff somewhat uncharitably.

"Yes but Hells Bells, no-one knew she was there before except the boy, and he's long gone", commented H.B.

"Quite right H.B.", said Bill quickly "No-one knew, and so nothing could be done, but now four someones know, and something can be done to help".

"To help, what can be done to help someone who has been dead this long", asked Griff, already fearing that he had read Bill's mind.

"Now boys", said Bill adopting his teachers persona once again, "I have known about this story a little longer than you and I've had more time to think, and I reckon we can help this poor girl's spiritual soul, by bringing her out of the stable and seeing her buried properly in the Chapel cemetery."

Bill's statement affected the atmosphere in the room. Strange how words which are only co-ordinated sounds, can affect the temperature in either direction, in this particular case it was up, and beads of perspiration which had been shining on top lips and foreheads began to join together and run.

Griff's voice a barely concealed shout split the air.

"NO", he cried and surprised by his own volume, modified his speech somewhat, trying to calm himself down, 'I mean I don't think that there is any point, there will be little or nothing left to find surely, after all this time, all that work for nothing". A sudden idea struck him,

"How about putting a plaque on false headstone, that would have some effect wouldn't it". He looked around unsuccessfully for support; the others were looking at him somewhat unbelievingly.

Tom Parry spoke kindly but firmly.

"Griff, this is unlike you, Good God, you have let people stay here that I would not let in through my garden gate, and here we have a little waif and stray, looking for some eternal comforts, and you are turning her down out of hand. Let's have a look and see if we can do something, I know that I could never have any peace of mind knowing that I had done nothing at all. Perhaps it's not her we'll be helping, but ourselves, so that we can live with our own consciences".

Griff knew he was beaten, if he continued to deny them, he would lose their friendship, and nothing was worth more than that.

"You are probably right Tom", he said resignedly, "When shall we do it then, Sunday would seem appropriate, I suppose, there are lots of tools out there we can use anyway".

"Sunday it is then", said Tom standing up, bringing the emotional session to a conclusion. They dispersed home then, each man anticipating with trepidation, the actions they were about to take.

Sunday morning duly arrived, and the quartet gathered at Griff's stable in the backyard of the pub. They were not happy men, rather nervous and expectant none had slept well. They looked as if they were waiting to enter the Dentist's surgery, for some group extraction, or drilling scheme. Eventually Griff led the way, unlocked the padlocked door, pushed it open, and they all trudged inside.

The stable was of lean-to construction, the back wall being the boundary wall of the Pub. The front wall door and one small, dirty, cobwebbed window looked into the yard, the blank side walls, and slated roof completed the somewhat inhospitable building. Looking about him at the flagstone floor, and brick stalls, of which there were four, now filled with assorted jumble, accumulated over many years.

"I'm glad I was never a horse, and put out here on a cold winter's night," commented Tom

"Hells Bells no, just imagine it, damp, wet with the wind whistling under that door," H.B. shuddered.

They both spoke rather nervously, and rather out of having to say something to try and relax the atmosphere, which was stiffening by the minute.

"'Where do we start", Griff who appeared to be suffering the jitters more than the other three, spoke quickly, in an almost falsetto tone before his voice recovered its normal baritone vibrato. "Well having thought about this all night, as we all probably have" Griff condescended, "I think the logical place to start is in the corner by the window".

"What brings you to that conclusion Griff", enquired Bill.

"Well, the stable has four corners, one of which is taken up by the door, and one is directly opposite the door, that discounts both of those. I think he would have wanted to keep an eye out for anyone approaching, so that he could stop working and hide if necessary". Griff's theory was plausible.

"Hells Bells that's good thinking, Griff, save us messing about", H.B. was always ready to follow the leader.

"Yes but isn't it just as logical, to take the furthest corner from the front, to cut down on the noise, or movement that could be seen or heard from outside", countered Bill Francis ever the bloody teacher.

"That's good thinking too Bill, Hells Bells, I don't know which way to go now", H.B. did a Stan Laurel impression in scratching his head.

Griff was not to be thwarted; he uplifted a pick, inserted the point under a flagstone in the near front corner, heaved up the flag, and said sternly, "We'll start here".

The men came forward recognising Griff's obstinacy, and started loosening and shovelling, glad of something to do to occupy themselves albeit bringing the dreaded moment of possible discovery nearer.

After about half an hour, an area of some four feet square had been cleared, and they started to dig down, working in pairs in the old mining tradition digging and clearing. No-one spoke, each had his own neurosis, deeper they went, sweating and panting, their ages beginning to tell. All exertions halted, when Tom's pick hit something that was neither stone nor soil. The point of his pick had actually stuck into something it was a wooden board, sodden with moisture after years in the ground.

"H.B. clear the earth from this board', commanded Tom. H.B. responded, and another board came into view, and a third, he looked up, "Well Griff it looks as if your theory was right".

They all stood round and looked down hesitantly.

"Come on then", said Tom softly "Let's get it over with".

With the edge of a shovel, he forced the boards apart, and raised them one after another. Under them were layers of what had once been hessian sacking, long since rotted, and Tom scraped gently with the shovel, and removed them. Using the shovel as accurately, and as gently as a surgeon's scalpel, he exposed some bones, and with the rest of the men looking down, in a heady mixture of wonderment, excitement and reverence, the whole skeleton was revealed.

Tom had been working in an almost hypnotic stare, not thinking of what actions he was taking. Then a voice from above snapped him back into reality. Griff's voice was an incredulous shout,

"Tom it's a dog, it's a bloody dog's skeleton, it's not a human shape at all". Tom gazed and sat on the edge of the hole they had dug.

"You're right Griff, it is a dog", he said, and smiled, the smile became a chuckle, the chuckle to a roaring laugh, as the tension that had pent up inside them all burst like dam. They all laughed, and guffawed, at the realisation that they would not, after all, be removing the bones of some long dead child, with all the trauma and emotion that would entail.

After some minutes of hysteria, they calmed down and began to wonder how they had been led to believe, that here they would find human remains. All faces turned to the translator of the manuscript.

Bill Francis looked a little sheepish, and was forced to confess, "Boys, this was obviously my mistake, but, in my own defence, it's only now with the evidence before us that I realise how I made that error. In the book the boy refers to the object of his affections as she, or her, never by name. I made the natural assumption that this was a girl. Finding her in an alley should have been a clue I suppose, but my knowledge of the language is more conversational than grammatical, and any way, none of you seemed to question it", he challenged them good naturedly.

"Hells Bells Bill, we thought you were the bloody expert" countered H.B.

"Never mind, all's well that ends well", said Tom, "Our consciences are clear, we did find out what was here, and would have done the right thing, had it been necessary, but thanks to Griff's logic theory, or downright luck", they all laughed at Tom's cheeky remark, "We found out quickly, we could have been here all day".

"Yes" said Griff now looking very relaxed "Let's replace the earth, leave the poor dog to its last resting place, clean up and have a drink, I think we all deserve one".

They readily agree, and completed the task of clearing up, replaced the flagstones and retired to the back room of the Pub.

After a few drinks, and some innocent banter at Bill Francis's fanciful translation, they made rather more serious promises of secrecy, lest they be thought the biggest fools in the Valley. The party of friends disbanded, and with and heads held in the position of men that had done their duty, returned to their homes.

Griff however was restless, and he returned to the room where he had found the old school exercise book. It was only days ago, but seemed like an age.

It had not been logic or luck that had made him choose the right corner to dig. It was because he knew what lay in the other corner, for he had put them there. He had killed his faithless wife and the soldier that night, and had put them in the far corner under the flagstones.

He had been severely frightened that his friends would not have listened to his arguments about where to dig, but he had been prepared for them to find the bodies, knowing that he would have received their understanding. However it had not come to it, and he was pleased his resolve had not been tested.

For the first time since the Brewery Architect had pronounced his sentence on the Station Hotel, Griff looked forward to the changes, he felt older, but more secure.

The back yard and stables were to be demolished and covered over, the space was to be used as a car park, and he could live on knowing his secret would be safe forever.

THE LETTER

There it stood on the mantelpiece propped up against the old wooden, square faced chiming clock which stood in the centre, a place of prominence that demanded attention. The letter that I had been waiting for, in fact the whole family had been waiting patiently for.

This was a message that was going to have a huge impact on my life, positive or negative.

The dreaming spires of Oxford, my personal dream beckoned, or possibly not.

The envelope had my name emblazoned on the front, for some reason I had almost expected it to be hand-delivered by a man wearing a mortar board and gown rather than our own normal postman. Ridiculous I know but such was the nature of my expectation. Anyway it was here.

I was not blessed with natural talent like some of my peers, I knew to achieve my goal I would have to work, study, and sacrifice part of my young life in doing so. I did this with open eyes and little reluctance. There were precious few nights out, holidays, or interaction with girls, such was my determination to be the first in my family to attend this fabled university.

I did sometimes wonder whether it would all be worth- while, but it appeared to me if I could achieve the acceptance to attend the university my future would be assured.

The sacrifices my parents and family had made and would have to continue to make also weighed heavily on my mind.

I had obtained the necessary grades and the interviews had gone well I thought, but that was no indication as there had been many others attending at the same time.

Now among the simple folds of paper contained within this envelope, this letter, lay the future direction of my life.

What if it was rejection, what then, another university a lesser one would beckon, I was not sure I could countenance it, it was Oxford or nothing, I was shooting for the moon.

My Mother came and sat in her chair by the fire. Her face calm and resolute, her hands folded in her lap. My Father joined her, standing behind the chair one hand on her shoulder, a picture of solidarity. Success would be met with joy, failure with compassion.

Waiting was over, time to look upon the signpost to my future.

I reached out with slightly trembling fingers, and butterflies doing somersaults in my stomach. Picking it up I quickly looked at my parents, my Father nodded approvingly.

Tearing open the envelope seemed almost sacrilegious but this was no time for hesitation. Taking out the white folded sheet from within I unfolded it until the contents were available and started to read the correspondence.

Dear Mr. Williams it began. We are sorry to have to inform you that your dental appointment for the 25th has had to be cancelled due to the indisposition of your dentist. We will re-arrange this appointment and inform you as soon as possible of the new date.

For a moment I could not understand it, they were not the words I has expected to read and so re-read them two or three times before the realization hit home.

My Father seeing my confusion stepped forward took the letter from me and read it, and passed it on to my Mother.

The release of tension in the room was palpable as we looked at one another and started to laugh. The ridiculous contradiction of the contents compared to the importance that we had expected was total.

My Mother did the only thing possible to return to normal she made a cup of tea.

The problem now was that the pressure would begin to rebuild awaiting the real letter to arrive this had only been a rehearsal.

THE LOOK

I timed the collision carefully. We collided in the department store doorway, she coming out and me ostensibly going in. I had no intention of entering the premises the meeting was the whole thing.

"Oh sorry" I said feinting to the right of her as if intending to go around.

"That's all right" she replied automatically without really looking up.

"Good grief Gaynor is it you ?" I asked with surprise in my voice. I knew of course exactly who she was as I had been watching and following her for some time.

Now she had to look, raising her eyes and smile in expectant hope.

"Yes, who.. Oh God it's Stephen isn't it ?" she stammered trying unsuccessfully to be pleasantly surprised. "Gosh it's been years", the smile froze on her crimson lips and never reached her brown and amber speckled eyes.

There it was, that look that I have seen in the eyes of so many women, the look of disdain, disapproval and frankly disgust.

But as far as I can remember she was the first, which was a shame because as a teenager I had idolised her. I had the "Full Monty" about her that you read about in books, I couldn't sleep without dreaming about her, lost my appetite, the whole thing, a complete infatuation.

My golden- haired, brown- eyed girl with a body to match her looks. Somehow I had finally persuaded her to come out with me but when I tried to kiss her, there it was, that look. I think it ignited the fire in my gut.

That was it. We saw each other about locally but she kept her distance. Her friends, no doubt due to her opinions, all gave me that look. In fact most of the women that I have managed to get close to sooner or later seem to adopt it.

I have learned to accept the fact that I am unattractive to the female of the species, deciding some time ago to address the now burning hate lying deep inside for the women that have rejected me.

I have thought long and hard and remembered over-hearing Great Aunt Grace talking about me to my Mother.

"Well, you have to admit dear there is something of a rodent about him".

Aunt Grace was the first to experience my wrath, and is no longer with us. She was a simple case because I knew exactly where she was at all times, she being very old and disabled. Using her own feather pillow, some firm pressure, goodbye Aunt Grace. No problem.

The next was Joanne, a friend of Gaynor's actually. She wasn't much of a difficulty either, being known locally as a drunken slut, not only by me but most people in the neighbourhood. A flight of concrete steps and a strong push from behind was all it needed. She never knew who it was. No-one really missed her apart from Pub landlords and her occasional customers.

Now however here's Gaynor. The others had really been rehearsals leading up to her. She had presented much more of a problem as she had married and moved away, but I have enjoyed the challenge.

Finding her turned out to be relatively straightforward if you knew how to do it. The secret was keeping it secret, no-one was to know. My one big advantage was my job, I am currently a postman and so I was able to intercept her Mother's mail. Steam it, read it and deliver it one day later who was to know, the post isn't what it was now is it.

Finding that she now lived in Bristol was O.K. too, as on my days off and at weekends I am a self-employed parcel courier with my own white van, what else. I am therefore able to move about quite anonymously, who looks at another white van.

Following her, finding where she lived and worked how she travelled to work, where and what her shopping habits were, it was all quite exciting. All the while the memory of that look burned inside. All leading to today's accidental coming together.

"Yes too many years to count" I replied laughingly, I actually knew it was Fifteen years and Eight months. "What are you doing now" I asked, knowing perfectly well her whole present life.

She looked at me her mouth going up and down nothing coming out. I had caught her cold as planned.

"Have you got time for a coffee and a quick catch up, there's a Starbucks next door" I interjected quickly. She still flapped but I knew that's where she was going anyway, she was not meeting anyone because she never did on a Thursday.

"Great" I enthused taking her arm more in guidance that anything else and strode into the coffee shop.

The following twenty minutes was great fun watching her squirm trying to find a reason to get away. She had aged somewhat in the intervening years. She obviously tried to maintain her appearance, make-up, hair colouring that sort of thing. However she had put on quite a few pounds, her plumper face took away her previous high cheek-boned look.

I looked at her and thought what the Hell did I ever see in you anyway, but the memory of that look raised the magma level in my inner volcano and I know she has no ultimate escape.

The enjoyment fell away and I allowed her the opportunity to get away on the pretext of catching the bus, although I knew her car was just two streets away. She always drove in on Thursdays, Saturdays she caught the bus.

I returned home to make final plans for Gaynor.

My wife, yes my wife for I did have someone who did not give me that look. I had chosen carefully, she was blind. Women of Gaynor's type would probably say "She would have to be". Be that as it may we had been married for three years now and it had begun well but had recently gone downhill.

In truth I have begun to tire of her constant complaining about things going wrong in the house, and my not being around to take care of them and her. I could not be out working and be at home now could I. Well I had taken an initial step in this regard.

This time it was the gas boiler that had packed up and there was no heating or hot water. On and on she went about how she could not manage without it, what was I going to do, she wanted it sorted out immediately. I'm afraid she chose a wrong moment, making statements when I had not long come through the door, demanding answers. Something snapped and I slapped her, unfair I know but I had to shut her up for a while I had to think. She was quiet after that.

I rang my mother who lived a short distance away, did she know of anyone who might take a look at the boiler as soon as possible. Yes she did. I knew she would my mother was pretty bright, liked to read the newspapers local and national cover to cover, kept up with all the news.

Her boiler had been serviced quite recently by a local firm Father and Son type of business plumbers etc. She gave me the number. A man answered and agreed to come round the following day. I explained that I could not be there but my wife, albeit blind I explained, knew where everything was.

I had to go back to Bristol after my Post job, I had to be seen regularly in Gaynor's area not raise any suspicions when the time came and it was coming soon.

On my return home there was a note from the engineer as to what was wrong with the boiler how much it might be to replace it as it was an old one. I exploded at the price and rang them back, telling them not give me the old story trying to get me to buy a new one surely they could repair it.

The engineer a younger man than I had spoken to previously, probably the son, explained they could use other parts but would not guarantee it lasting, it should be replaced. I said to repair it. He reluctantly agreed but it would take several visits as he would have to locate parts. I agreed.

I did not need this aggravation, just now my head was racing with plans for Gaynor.

I decided that Tuesday would be the day. It was her afternoon off and mid afternoon the neighbourhood would be quiet when most people would be at work.

I prepared carefully. I had false number plates attached to the van. I wore a pair of dark blue overalls, a hi-viz vest with another company's logo on. I had stolen this from another courier some time back in preparation for this day, baseball cap, glasses I did not need, and most importantly latex gloves. To complete the impression I had also made a small cardboard box full of fresh air to deliver. I was ready, it was time, the magma was boiling.

I pulled up at her door, jumped out holding my mobile phone up to my ear as a further obstacle to seeing my face should anyone be looking from behind net curtains. I was just a delivery man.

I rang the bell and waited, I could see her shape approaching the door through the frosted glass panel. The door opened two inches and I shoulder charged it. The door slammed back against her knocking her down. I was quickly inside closing the door behind me and was on her in a flash.

No pleasantries this time, Vesuvius was exploding. My hands found her throat and the look in her eyes before the light went out was surprise and fear. No more looking now you bitch.

It was all over in minutes. In some ways I was disappointed it was over so quickly. I should have made it last longer and maybe see her plead. It would not have done any good so possibly it was better this way.

I dragged her into the lounge laying her on a settee, arranging her to look as if she was sleeping. I checked around straightened anything that looked askew, picked my box and left.

I drove cautiously away, no high revs or wheel spin now. Checked my watch, it had taken twenty minutes. Hopefully not long enough to be suspicious. Stopping at a secluded spot on an industrial estate I took off my disguise and it all went into an opaque black bag and I sealed it. It was going to a landfill site as soon as possible.

It had all been quite erotic, the excitement of the discovery and chase, the build up of the day and the final explosive and releasing act, it had been wonderful. Finally as I drove home, observing every speed limit and the highway- code to the letter. I realized that I could do it again and again with any woman of my choice. I had the power.

Approaching home I wondered what she was going to complain about today. It had been some weeks since the boiler incident, and after some visits by the engineer the boiler seemed to be working fine, a few hiccups but that was to be expected.

I pulled onto the hard standing next to the bungalow and noticed there were no lights on. This was not unusual as she obviously did not need them, but she normally put them on when I was expected back. Then I remembered the events of the day had put it out of mind. She had arranged to spend the day at my Mother's, I couldn't remember why.

Entering by the kitchen in quite high spirits, I called her name just in case she had returned, and switched on the light, there was a bright flash.

The local newspaper headlines shouted "Bungalow Completely Destroyed By Gas Explosion, One Man Killed".

The verdict of the inquest was Death by Misadventure after the evidence of the engineers stating the poor condition of the boiler in the house. They had written copies of the warnings given, and telephone recordings of the refusal by the customer to replace it. They had done all they could but ultimately the boiler had failed. Gas had leaked and built up, any spark such as an electrical switch could cause an explosion, and it did.

Family and friends commiserated with the widow. Her solicitor informed her that her husband had as recently as last year taken insurance was fully paid and would cover a rebuild. She moved in with her mother-In-law whilst the work was carried out.

One day some weeks later sitting alone in the garden, her mobile phone rang. The voice did not identify itself although she knew full well who it was.

"All went well, be with you very soon now, love you!"

It was David the engineer and her lover. She had traced his face with her fingers.

She had liked the look of him.

Stuart Kear

THE MESSENGER

Huw Stratford was a bachelor who lived alone in the house where he had been brought up, his parents' house or more correctly his Grand Parents house. His father had been killed in the war when he was a child, his Grandfather years before in a mining accident. Consequently he had been raised by his mother, and she had passed away some years before bequeathing the house to him as her only child. He had a steady little job at the tubular steel furniture factory and life was comfortable, if at times a little lonely and a little empty. He was happy enough but felt that maybe life could have a little more to offer. What that little more was he had up to this point not been able to discover.

However of late he had noticed a new lady serving in the canteen at the factory. Truthfully he had noticed her because she seemed to be constantly looking at him. Every time he looked up there she was pointedly looking in his direction. He could not understand it. He did not feel attracted to her in any sort of romantic way and yet there was something about her that intrigued him

It was somewhat disquieting for him; he thought he had left all that sort of thing behind. Not that the female of the species had figured large on his curriculum vitae, apart from his mother of course. She stood like the Statue of Liberty and he had loved and cared for her until the day she died.

He realized the situation could not go on in this fashion he must approach her or ignore her. The way he felt he did not think that the latter was achievable she was already under his skin, rather like an itch he could not reach to scratch. Therefore somehow or other he had to at least initially speak to her, try to ascertain what if any, her interest was in him.

He had spoken confidentially to friends who were encouraging him onward, dropping hints such as they had heard she had been enquiring about him. Could he believe them or was this just men talk. He just wished he'd had more experience with the opposite sex. What if she rejected his advance saying that the eye-catching had all been coincidental and smiles had only been civil rather than friendly.

He had to try.

Next lunchtime he moved along in the queue until he stood facing her. He looked deep into her green eyes and said,

"Hello my name is Huw"

"Yes I know" she replied confidently "my name is Lauren" he was about to reply when a voice from behind in the line said

"Oi, come on Huw stop trying to chat up the staff we are all waiting to be served"

"I, I, wasn't trying……"

She was now smiling broadly, he hurriedly moved on.

He was getting nowhere at this rate he thought. Next time he started quickly with

"Look I wasn't trying to chat you up or whatever it's called".

She completely threw him with

"Yes you are and you are not very good at it are you" she stated. He looked at her dumbfounded. She continued "So here is what we are going to do. Meet me outside the Cross Keys tonight at half past seven. You know the pub ?" she asked a completely shell shocked Huw.

"Y. Yes I do" he stumbled.

"Right good, see you tonight then" she smiled dismissively and turned to serve the next customer.

Huw felt he had been hit by a truck in the nicest possible way. Shock, excitement bewilderment all washed over him in turn. She had not asked him, she had told him. He simply could not get over it. He would have to by tonight.

He checked his watch he was bang on time, seven thirty on the dot. Looking around she was for the moment not to be seen. Oh God he thought I hope this is not a wind up, she had seemed quite definite. He stood there feeling like a teenager on a first date wondering how on earth this was going to turn out, hands shoved deep into his trouser pockets, uncertainty creeping over him like a shroud. Should he just go home, all the open ended questions held him fast. At least it wasn't raining he thought.

The sound of heels click-clacking like castanets made him turn. Here she came out of the semi-darkness of the car park into the golden light flooding from the windows of the pub. She was smartly dressed in a three-quarter length red coat over black trousers with a multi coloured scarf around her neck and shoulders. She carried a black handbag large enough to be a briefcase. Her brown hair looked somewhat different. He realized then that he had only ever seen her in the canteen uniform and so her appearance was bound to be altered. A partial sense of relief passed over him, at least he was not going to be stood up.

"Hello Huw sorry to be a little late" she started a little breathlessly "I had to park the car a little further away than I expected".

The use of his Christian name seemed just a little familiar as he felt they had not really met before, only over the counter at the cafeteria, but he let it pass.

"That's O.K. I've only just arrived myself so I've not actually waited" he replied.

"Oh good, that's all right then shall we go in" she pushed at the door and entered without waiting for him to answer.

He felt once again that she was taking the lead. He was not used to it and wasn't sure whether he liked it or not, he was used to taking the decisions in his life but then, it was only him wasn't it.

The Pub was relatively quiet and so they had the choice of places to sit. She walked forward to a corner seat with a table and sat down once again he felt he was trailing in her wake. Taking off her coat she looked around Huw decided that she was not going to order the bloody drinks as well and quickly asked what she wanted. A glass of dry white wine she smiled the answer. At least I got in first with that he thought.

Returning to the table with his Pint of beer and her glass of wine he sat next but not close to her as this was still strange territory for him.

"Right well, can we start with first things first" he was trying to be assertive now. "Here we are you know my name but I do not really know yours, shall we introduce ourselves".

"Yes, my name is Laura Standing and you are Huw Stratford, how do you do" she replied a little mockingly holding out her hand for him to grasp, he shook it gently.

He was becoming more aware of her accent which he decided was Northern, possibly Geordie or somewhere up there, he had not noticed in the general hullaballoo of the canteen. He still could not deny a certain sense of foreboding within him. He felt as if he was sitting in the dentist chair awaiting a procedure.

"What are you doing in the valleys of South Wales, you are a long way from home" he ventured cautiously taking the first step into the minefield.

"Looking for someone" she replied mysteriously, smoothing down her trousers.

"Anyone in particular or just a general look-about" he asked trying to lighten his ever darkening senses.

"No, someone in particular, in fact you" she stated flatly her eyes never leaving his face.

He sat back astounded.

"Why on earth would you come looking for me" he asked somewhat suspiciously.

"Before I explain I want to show you some pictures" she said putting the large black handbag on her lap, opening it and removing a small file with papers and photographs.

"Any idea who this might be," she asked putting a sepia coloured photograph of a young smiling soldier in uniform on the table.

He picked it up looked at it carefully, there was something there but not really.

"No" she said "How about these two", the second was of a couple on their wedding day, the bride in a long white gown the same soldier in uniform.

He now took out his glasses staring at the old black and white, bent and battered photograph.

"I think that's my Mother" he exclaimed "Who, who is that, is that my father" he asked incredulously.

"Have you never seen these images before" she asked gently her eyes softening.

"Never" He replied not taking his eyes off the photographs on the table.

"My Mother always said that he had been killed in the last days of the war and there had been no pictures of him, and there had been no cameras around when they got married. I always assumed that was the case and never thought any more about it. Plenty of other kids had no fathers after the war for the same reason. She never mentioned him and I always assumed that it was too painful for her and so I never questioned it" he explained.

"How about this one then" she fished out another black and white photograph. This contained patently the same man but with a different woman both in smart suits, he with a flower in his lapel and she carrying a small bouquet with a corsage on her lapel. The styles of the suits placed them in the late forties or early fifties he guessed.

"Look" he said defensively "I have never seen any of these things before, if that is my father who is the other woman my Mother would certainly have been alive when these pictures were taken."

"The people in the second picture were my parents" she said flatly.

The silence that followed was heavy with his bewilderment. He just stared at the images before him his brain trying to take in the implications.

"But you said your name was Standing" he managed to splutter.

"That was my married name, I will give you three guesses what my maiden name was" she answered.

" It; you; it cannot have been Stratford surely" he stammered.

"Oh but it was" came her reply.

He was getting annoyed now as he was obviously at a huge disadvantage.

"Look you obviously know what's going on here. Let's start with him are you saying that is my father, a father I have never seen nor know anything about. How can you be so sure." He asked indignant now.

"Because he told me before he died" she responded.

"Oh and what else did he tell you" anger now rose in his throat he felt like a child being told something he should know but didn't.

"The whole story, his whole story" she said softly, leaning forward a little desperate to create a connection realizing how helpless he must feel.

He was not sure he wanted to hear the whole story, it appeared as if it would have an explosive effect on his quiet comfortable life.

"Just stay and listen, what you do after I have finished will be entirely up to you, but I promised him I would find you and explain everything". It was an emotional appeal her green eyes swam with the earnestness of wanting to fulfil her promise.

He looked down again at the photographs and then back up to her "Right, well you have come this far you had better get it off your chest".

She started by saying that his father had actually seen him on his last leave before going overseas, he had realized then that marrying your mother had been a terrible mistake for both of them. Your mother had become pregnant, they had to marry and they lived with your Grandmother. He says they were strong willed, controlling women, and his life would have been a misery. He wrote to your Mother telling her of his feelings, the war then overtook him.

He had been fighting in Germany and the Germans were fighting desperately. One day his unit were using an old building for cover when it and they received a direct hit from an artillery shell. When he awoke he was the only one left alive the others had been literally blown to bits, he had been wounded in the legs. He had lain there for some time when he noticed a set of I.D. discs laying in the mud, blown off some poor unfortunate soldier. Realizing that he had a chance to disappear, on an impulse he took off his identification and threw it away donning the set he had found.

He was eventually discovered and sent back to a field hospital and then back to England to recover, by the time he had the war was over. There was tremendous confusion then with men returning, he waited to be de-mobbed. Using this new identity he went North where he knew there was coal mining found a job and stayed. He reverted to his original surname changing only his Christian name knowing by this time that he had been officially declared Missing In Action like thousands of others. He met and married my Mother whom he loved, and they stayed married for Thirty years or more, I am the result.

He never regretted leaving your Mother but he did very much regret leaving you.

There, she said were the bare bones of the story none of which she was aware of until her father's final days.

She sat back and took a drink of her wine her eyes scanning his face trying to anticipate what his reactions were going to be.

He simply sat there inert, his brain bubbled like a coffee percolator trying to absorb all this information.

"Listen" he said at last "I think I need some fresh air and a little walk, do you want another drink".

She did, he got her one and went and stood outside letting the cool evening air calm the turbulence in his head. He walked into and around the car park and returned.

"I am going to need a little time to think about all this, but just off the top of my head have you considered some of the implications here, if this got out" he stated.

"Yes, I have known about this for a while now, legally he was a bigamist and I am illegitimate, but they were my parents he was my

Dad and you are my half-brother. They are the salient facts, I doubt if anybody else would want to know, this is a family matter. Too much time has elapsed for there to be any relevance to any-one else."

She finished speaking and rummaged in her bag coming up with a writing pad and pen.

"I am returning to Sunderland, I have fulfilled my promise to my Father, here is my address and telephone number there, should you decide you want to contact me. I completely understand your confusion all I ask is that you don't shoot the messenger."

She stood, gathered her coat and bag, and as she passed, smiled and kissed him on the cheek. Then she was gone.

He swallowed what was left of his drink which constituted a record for the longest time he had ever taken to drink one pint of beer.

It took many days of contemplation before he reached a conclusion.

Huw was not going to allow this anonymous old man who was trying to salve his conscience in his dying days affect him.

It was by the merest chance of sperm meeting egg that caused his birth. He was his father only because that was the technical name given to the male producer of the sperm. He would never think of him as his Dad as that was an emotional term and had to be earned by love and commitment none of which had been forthcoming.

Huw would also never let anything nor anyone contradict the love and opinions he had of his Mother who had fully met and surpassed the terms and conditions needed to be called by that name.

The incident was over. The knowledge would be locked away in the drawer marked "Experience" in his head. The only positive to emerge was that he had a Sister and he liked the sound of that. He looked at the sheet of paper she had given him and remembered the affectionate kiss. She was as much an innocent here as he.

He would give her a call. Sunderland wasn't that far away.

Stuart Kear

THE DEPARTURE

Simon walked along the station subway. He had been loath to leave the warmth and leather-seated comfort of his Porsche 911 Boxter.

A damp cold wind blew open his Burberry raincoat and ruffled his well- cut fair hair. He turned and trudged up the steps to the platform above. The wind was stronger as he neared the top, and it carried spots of rain, telling him as if he didn't already know, what the weather was doing outside.

Standing at the top of the steps, he looked at the almost deserted platform. It was glistening wet from the rain driven in under the station roof. Empty crisp packets and bits of newspapers flew about, settling untidily in sheltered nooks and crannies. Bedraggled pigeons perching in the cast iron rood supports sheltered from the elements, everything else just dripped.

There were hardly any human beings to be seen, just one or two station staff scurrying about their tasks, hunched against the wind and rain.

Simon pushed back his crisp white shirt cuff to check the time on Rolex Oyster watch. Her train would be leaving in twenty minutes. Was she already here, he would have to check. She was obviously not on the platform itself.

He scoured the waiting-room, chock full of steaming humanity, everyone dressed in Anoraks, raincoats and hats, with umbrellas leaking and forming little pools on the floor.

Although tall he had to stand on the tips of his toes to look over the people in the front but could not see her in there, thank God.

The cafeteria was similarly full and uncomfortably hot, she was not here either. He decided to have a cup of coffee whilst he waited it seemed the least onerous of the waiting areas. There was table where he could sit apart from the other people.

"Terrible weather" he ventured to the girl who served him, just making condescending conversation. He was consumed by his own thoughts, and of what he was about to do and say.

"Tell me about it" the girl replied. A wisp of hair had escaped from under her hat. She wiped it away with a hand that exposed broken, badly-painted fingernails and cheap sovereign rings. He shuddered. "Good for business though" she added sweeping her hand now in the direction of the crowds gathered inside, most consuming something or other.

I'm glad somebody's happy, Simon thought patronisingly, as he turned away. The door opened, the wind blew in and was quickly shut out. The windows were steamed up, but the raindrops dribbling down the outside were still visible.

A train arrived, and the temperature in the cafeteria dropped as people left.

Walking over, he checked up and down, nothing.

As he closed the door he worried about the effect his words might have on her.

Would she collapse in tears, shout and scream making a scene of some kind. She could be vulnerable. He hoped it would not prove to be embarrassing for him. He would be as gentle with her as he could.

Five minutes later she arrived. Her arrival coinciding with mumble of the station announcer, his robotic voice lost in the wind.

Simon stood and went to her.

Suzanne was a very attractive woman of a certain age, well dressed in a white military style raincoat, belt tied at the waist, collar up and her long dark hair tucked inside. In her black fashionably high- heeled shoes, inappropriate for the weather but an essential part of her style, she clicked across the floor causing some stares, as was always the point.

He asked her to sit at the table and whether she wanted coffee. She declined. He began quickly. There was no time left, it had to be ended here and now.

"Suzanne, I'm sorry I had to ring you at work but I had no other choice. I knew you were leaving for Manchester tonight and I had to explain". He stumbled over his words.

"You have no need to explain, I understand completely. I am too old for you Simon, does about sum it up" she asked coldly, her voice reflected in her icy blue eyes.

"Put like that it sounds rather horrible" he replied, taken aback with the correctness of her assessment. Angela had assured him the Suzanne would never know. Evidently she did know. She sat quite still, straight backed, and looked at him for a long unblinking moment, her hands with their long manicured fingers laced together in her lap.

"Simon, you are a weak, spoiled and unimaginative young man. You have allowed yourself to be influenced by another younger woman. I could have given everything you would ever need and more. I would have made a man of you, but you have made your choice, her above me". She strove to contain the tears that threatened to fall.

She kept her voice flat and hard, desperate for him not to hear the tremor that would betray her inner turmoil.

Suzanne had discovered his betrayal by over-hearing a work colleague's bitchy remark about her relationship with Simon. Something along the lines of her being old enough to be his mother, toy boy, what was she thinking of, there could be no future in it, surely he must have friends of his own age etc. etc.

She began looking for small signs of his deception and found them. Sudden cancelling of arrangements, dates, weekends, hastily stopping mobile phone conversation, unanswered text messages and some obvious lies.

She followed him and soon discovered his meetings with Angela, a beautiful young advertising executive. Suzanne was devastated.

She had been so certain of him she had seen her future with him. Without him her future looked bleak and lonely. She had tried to change him, to persuade him into other areas of life, but obviously she had failed.

She had to go change her surroundings start again. She was strong she'd find another, move on. Seeing him know however doubts began to crystalize, could she find another. She felt just a sliver of fear that it was too late for her.

His call at work had surprised her. She had hoped to have left without seeing him, to avoid this confrontation. Seeing him made it immeasurably more difficult, still she would see it through.

Although her emotions screamed at her to hold the face she loved in her hands and kiss him, make him change his mind, she knew it was a false hope.

Her words were a body blow for Simon. He thought he held all the cards. He had hoped Suzanne would have begged him to stay, keep him at any price. He had secretly thought he could have kept Suzanne in the background whilst he married Angela. Angela's father was a senior partner in a large City brokers, and that was where he saw his future. He spluttered some excuses in reply to her ultimatum.

She stood, gathered he handbag over her shoulder and said "You could at least see me off". Not waiting for a reply she turned away.

He murmured sheepishly, "Of course", picking up her small suitcase, extending the handle and pulling it behind him, followed on the platform where the cold, wet wind hit them again.

She moved to the front of the platform as the train appeared a little distance away. The announcer intoned the destination and people drifted forward.

She had turned away quickly in the cafeteria because she had lost the battle with her tears and now they flowed freely as she kept her back to him. The train approached.

She turned to him suddenly; eyes wide and desperate now, crying "Kiss me Simon". He put down her suitcase and walked towards her.

They embraced. She had her arms around him inside his unbuttoned coat and, as the kiss lingered, she gripped him tighter. Suddenly she pivoted on one foot throwing her weight backward pulling them off the edge of the platform into the path of the on-coming train.

THE LEARNING GAME

"Stand still fat man or you're dead", Gordon's top two fingers were the barrel of a Colt 45 pointed directly at an unfortunate mongrel dog that had just happened to cross our path. His thumb being the gun's hammer wavered for a second before falling in perfect time with his exclamation, "Bam, gotcha, I told you not to move didn't I". He puffed the imaginary smoke from his chubby dirty fingers.

The shaggy brown dog looked up momentarily wagging his tail, surprised by the shout. Now realising that nothing more was to follow it gave us a derisory yellow-eyed look that had "Blooming kids" written on them and he ambled on his way.

It was Saturday morning, Gordon and lived in Dodge City, Ton Pentre, on the way home after seeing a Cowboy Western at the local cinema. We walked slowly, bandy legged, hands hanging menacingly over a pair of pearl handled short legged trouser pockets, two scruffy nine-year old hard cases just looking for trouble and more than ready to sort it out.

Unfortunately Saturday lunch-time in Ton Pentre at that time was pretty peaceable. People were more interested in shopping at the Co-op and Hutchings the butchers than trying to shoot it out with two gun-fighters on the run from the law, and anyway everybody knew who we were.

"Oh hello David", said a woman coming out of the Post Office. She was lucky we didn't gun her down surprising us like that, "Tell your Mother I'll see her about four o'clock.

"Hello Mrs. Harris", I said a little sheepishly, looking down at my Fairisle jumper, wondering if she had noticed out game, "Yes O.K. I'll tell her".

"Hey Gord", I ventured "Let's go home the gully way, we can gallop then without anyone getting in the way" He agreed and we ran home slapping out backsides in alternate time with our black dapped feet making the satisfying sound of a three legged horse.

My Mother had lunch ready on the table when I arrived home, egg and chips, proper food for an action man. She knew that the afternoon would be a marathon game of cowboys and Indians across the coal tips and mountains behind our house, and a man would need feeding up for that. I told her between mouthfuls about Mrs. Harris.

Gordon and I would meet anyway, but as always most of the other kids had been to the Cinema too and had the same idea. We would gather as if led by the Pied Piper to the street corner by the old wooden telegraph pole. The meeting place for all games and plans.

Sides would be chosen. Almost everyone had some kind of costume and armaments. Silver six-guns in belts with holsters(normally Christmas or birthday present , jealously guarded), black waistcoats with yellow fringes and a shiny Sheriff's badge pinned on, some even had a matching hat, although that was sometimes seen as a step too far.

The assortment of weapons was impressive too, from rubber knives stuck in trouser belts with a snake clasp, wooden rifles made by Dads to pukka plastic rifles, bows and arrows made from local trees, a pretty fierce bunch we looked.

Gordon however always seemed to have the best weapon. Today he had his brother's air rifle, no pellets just the gun, but it made a really satisfying "KRAING" when he pulled the trigger after compressing the spring by breaking the barrel. Everyone wanted a try, but I was the only one he'd allow, after all I was his best friend

I was little nervous when holding it I must confess, but not Gord. In fact he liked nothing better that holding the gun as close as he could to someone's bare arm or leg pulling the trigger and laughing when the force of the air from the barrel made them jumped back in alarm.

His dark unruly hair would flop over his deep se blue eyes, as he searched for another victim.

The sunny warm afternoon flew by, if anyone won the game it didn't matter, we'd all been killed and re-born half a dozen times anyway. The voices of Mother's calling their respective children home for tea floated on the breeze and kids started to drift away. There was no denying those siren's calls.

Gordon never wanted to go home. "Let's hide and pretend we can't hear, let's stay until it's dark", he whispered as if anyone was listening. He was fearless, nothing seemed to scare him, it was this element of danger that drew me to him. However upsetting my Mother worried me more.

"Nah I got to go" I said "I'm starving anyway" which wasn't a lie. We trudged homeward, Gord's a half-step behind me for the first time in the day usually he was two steps in front.

"Look at the state of you, go and wash before your tea", usual comments from my Mother standing there in a wrap over pinny, whilst my silent father was listening to the wireless shouting the football results and checking on something mysterious called a "Pools Coupon".

"And why are you always the last home" she continued "Tony next door's been home for ages, it's that Gordon Williams isn't it. Why must you always play with him, he'll get you into trouble one day".

That's another reason why Gord' attracted me, my Mother didn't like him.

The next Saturday morning it was Errol Flynn in "Robin Hood" at the pictures. All the way home we shot imaginary arrows into everything and everyone sword fenced without swords until our arms ached.

The usual gang gathered later with bows and arrows with suckers on the end, wooden swords and the like. My grey shield and short sword was actually Roman but no-one cared. Gord' was a little late but when he arrived it was with murmurs of approval and shock.

He had a proper shop-bought bow, and a pointed steel tipped arrow.

"Cor' where did you get that from Gord'" I asked jealously reaching out just to touch it.

"It's my big brother Stan's old one, he's a member of the Archery Club and he won't miss it 'cause he's gone to watch the football" he said standing proudly showing it to everyone. The bow stood a foot taller than most of us. He began to bend it against the street gutter as he had seen his brother do, pushing the draw string up to the top notch. The bow was ready.

"Watch this" he commanded, loading the arrow. He pulled back the string a little and released it. The arrow flew the four or five feet between us and the thick wooden telegraph pole, thudding into the soft wood. Everyone laughed and said "Good Shot", God' seemed to grow in size as he walked forward to pull out the arrow.

This was something new we all knew that our toy weapons were really just that, toys, but this was something real. The bow and arrow took on an almost mystical significance. We also knew that if our parents found out there would be no game this afternoon and so we vanished into the hills all hoping Gord' would let us try the bow and arrow. He wouldn't, not even me.

I suppose in any group there is going to be one person that everyone else dislikes, so it is with Alan Llewellyn in our gang. We tolerate him because he lives on our street, but no-one really likes him. It is difficult to say why we dislike him, he's ordinary enough, but seems to think he's above everyone else, big headed I suppose. Alan is little older and taller than most of us, and tends to look as if he smells something nasty, when looking down his nose at you.

Gordon doesn't just dislike him he hates him for some reason and normally Alan keeps his distance, but today he joins in the game.

As usual we wander wherever the games take us, now we were having a pitched battle in some abandoned allotments. During the heat of the battle Alan turns from sword fencing one boy with their wooden swords and stabs at the next person in front. He realises to his horror that the striped T shirt belongs to Gordon. Gord' spins around to see who has had the nerve to stab in the back, his eyes narrow to navy blue slits when he recognises Alan.

One look into those hard eyes is enough. Alan knows that his punishment will be swift in coming and takes to his heels, running across the allotments. We all laugh as Gord' cries out,

"Alan stop running, come back or I'll shoot you with the bow".

Alan takes no notice. He thinks the nearer he gets to home the safer he will be, and carries on running.

"Alan stop or I will shoot you" shouts Gord'.

It's obvious to everyone that Alan isn't going to stop. Gord' looks about, unslings the bow which he had carried slung across his back as Errol Flynn had done. Pulling the arrow of his long grey sock with the two red bands around the top, he loads the arrow pulls back the draw string with all his already considerable ten year old strength, aims and fires.

Everything is happening in slow motion now as we all realise how good Gord's aim is. Alan appears to be running directly into the path of the metal pointed arrow, which has somehow enlarged itself for we can follow it clearly. Alan is approaching the disused gateway to the allotments still running hard. One of the two railway sleepers raised vertically to form the gate still stands.

Amazingly it is at this precise point that their paths collide, the only place in the old gardens where anything stands higher than a gooseberry bush. At the exact moment that Alan passed in front of the railway sleeper the arrow thudded into it at approximately neck height.

He shuddered to a halt, looked at the arrow, then further back at Gord' immediately taking in what might have happened. He uttered a cry and continued his journey home at even greater pace.

Time and sound returned to normal, we all looked around at one another, a nervous laugh here, a "Phew that was close" there. The game was over. The incident had been too close for comfort.

"I told him not to run didn't I, I warned him" Gord' spoke to no-one in particular as if looking for forgiveness or justification. He didn't receive any. We all know there is going to trouble for this action and we all shrink away from him, including me, all wanting to get home and safety.

The day had turned cold and Gord' was suddenly a lonely figure. No longer the brave leader, fighting at the front of his troops, now someone who could maybe lose control and commit an irresponsible act of revenge merely to maintain a certain reputation. He now slightly frightened me.

My Mother's words went through my mind. She could be right I thought.

THE VICAR'S WIFE

Mrs. Vanessa Watkins withdrew her pink gloved hands from the hot sudsy water of the kitchen sink. A knock at the side door of the Vicarage had interrupted her thoughts as she washed up the Royal Albert tea service, after the umpteenth meeting of the Friends of St. Dyfrig's
She removed the gloves, smoothed her dress and replaced a lock of brown hair that had escaped the clasp at the nape of her neck.

"Morning Mrs. Watkins", the weather beaten face of Charley the gardener cum handyman smiled respectfully when she opened the door. "I've come to make a start on the Rhododendrons".

"Morning Charley", she responded "Good, you know where everything is don't you". She waved a hand elegantly in the direction of the garden shed, "I'll bring you a cup of tea presently".

As she closed the door she noticed that Charley had an assistant today, a tall man with dark hair. Sensible really she thought, returning to the kitchen, some of the bushes were quite high.

The Rhododendron bushes had grown enormously since they had arrived here eight years ago. They were now starting to block the light into Jeffrey's study, encroaching onto the short drive and restricting the full use of the lawn to the side of the Vicarage, where summer events were traditionally held. She had mentioned this to Jeffrey last year but nothing had been done, which was not unusual. This year she decided to arrange it herself, hence Charley.

After putting the dishes away she stood leaning against the kitchen unit gazing out of the window, her melancholy mood persisted. How many more interminable coffee mornings, inconsequential meetings, bazaars, bring and buy sales, with well intentioned but ultimately boring people could she possibly attend. She was drowning, almost unable to remember who she was, or what if anything she'd ever wanted from life.

It had all been so different at University when she met Jeffrey. His faith, his enthusiasm, his belief that he could change the way people saw God had shone from him like a beacon. Like a moth to a flame she had been drawn. He had been irresistible. His long dark hair, long beard, the round Lennon glasses, the total unconcern for material things. His clothes were unkempt, he rarely ate properly, accounting for his rapier like slimness, creating an almost Christ like image. They had married immediately after graduating and the great crusade had begun.

Twenty years on, the light had gone out. Dimmed by the Church's refusal to change public apathy, social depravation. Jeffrey's enthusiasm had been seen as almost revolutionary and he was regularly placed in inner city parishes that would have knocked the zeal out of John the Baptist. He had lost as much of his faith as he had of his hair, his soul being as bare now as the top of his head. The only thing he had gained was weight, reminding her secretly of Mr. Pickwick. He found it necessary to visit religious retreats twice a year, attempting to rediscover his faith. His enthusiasm on returning would ebb away and he would become disconsolate and irritable, leaving her to take charge of Parish matters.

The catalyst for her reflective mood lay on the Dresser, a letter had arrived from an old college friend who had re-married and gone to live in America. They had kept in touch over the years, Christmas cards that sort of thing, but now this, a letter brimming with confidence extolling the wonders of American life containing an invitation to visit and experience these wonders. The enthusiasm in the writing beamed out, serving only to illuminate her own dull, dreary existence more forcibly. She longed to go, but how could she, how could she. In sheer frustration the letter was torn in half and thrown in the waste bin, there were things to do.

Late the next morning, catching up on some delayed paperwork she heard a knock on the kitchen door. There stood Charlie's helper holding a bloodied handkerchief to his left forearm.

He started "I'm sorry to disturb you, but I've had a little accident and wondered whether you would have such a thing as a plaster or something" his voice was low, his eyes soft brown and he had a Northern accent,

"Of course come in" she stood aside to let him pass "Whatever have you done"? There was an earthy, honest, manly smell as he passed her.

"It's nothing really", he said, as she motioned him to sit on the plain wooden chair at the kitchen table. " A branch I had just cut, sprung back and caught me under my forearm, I'm all right it's just that the blood is running down and dripping off my elbow making a bit of a mess."

"Let me have a look at it", she said returning from the cupboard with a small first aid kit. Holding his wrist she turned his arm over and took off the handkerchief. "Oh, it really is quite deep I can clean and bandage it, but I think you need to go the hospital to have it stitched".

As she worked and they chatted, she became more and more aware of his physical presence, the heat from his body, the firmness of his arm, the darkness of his hair. By the time she had finished, he declined her offer of a lift to the hospital, explaining he was quite capable of driving but that he was very grateful for what she had done, and quite quickly he had gone.

She stood, her head slightly swimming, feeling somewhat disorientated. He was a total stranger, and yet they had chatted with the ease of old friends, she had not even asked his name, it had not seemed necessary. Something deep inside her had not wanted him to leave.

"Vanessa, did you finish typing the notes for my address to the Seminar, I really do need them now", Jeffrey's slightly nasal tones were demanding. He walked into the Study, pushing his metal framed spectacles back up to the bridge of his perspiring nose with the tip of his forefinger. A habit she found increasingly annoying.

"Jeffrey, I told you yesterday I had finished them, they are in your briefcase", she was quite short with him, he was quite capable of typing his own notes, he just chose not to do so.

"Ah, yes" he said rifling through the briefcase and finding the file, there went the finger tip again, "Right, well that seems to be about everything, Um, Shaving Kit", he raised both eyebrows in her direction.

"In your toilet bag, in your suitcase, in your car", she said flatly, slightly exasperated at his absent mindedness.

"Well, I'll be off then, I leave everything in your capable hands, see you Friday, you've got the Hotel number if you want me", and of he bumbled with a final push to his glasses.

She went to the door to wave him off, neither expecting nor receiving a return to her wave. The car disappeared from view.

The grandfather clock in the hall struck the half hour past seven as she swung her legs up on to the leather pouffe, and sank back into the armchair a glass of red wine in her hand. Her television companion blinked in the corner, she watched with unseeing eyes. The front door bell rang jangling her nerves.

"Oh' God, who can this be now", she muttered, not really expecting an answer from the almighty.

Opening the door all she saw initially was a large bunch of flowers, beautiful in their arrangement and colours. A black haired, brown eyed face appeared from behind them with a shy embarrassed smile that created dimples in his cheeks.

"Oh' it's you", she said slightly startled, but undoubtedly pleased.

" Hello, yes it's me" he replied laughing "I just thought to say thank you for attending to my wounds the other day, and to show you that there's no lasting damage", he held up his arm, now professionally bound. "I have to go back to Leeds at the end of the week, and this might be the only chance I get to thank you", his smile was warm and sincere, as he held out the flowers.

"They are lovely, thank you, but it really was nothing", she hesitated continuing, "Would you like to come in while I put them in water".

"If you are sure I'm not disturbing you", he replied hesitatingly, his crisp white, short sleeved shirt, accentuating his tanned arms, face and neck the result of working outdoors. The hall light glinted off the golden hoop in his ear.

Her pulse was quickening, you are disturbing me somewhat, but not in the way you think, she thought.

"Of course not come on in", she said with a smile in her voice.

He passed her and she closed the door, this time he smelled fresh and clean.

"Go through into the lounge, I won't be a minute. Excuse the mess I wasn't expecting company this evening", the words just tumbled out of her mouth.

"Damn it I sound like a school girl, get a grip" she thought. Standing at the kitchen sink, water gurgling into a glass vase, she was aware of him close behind her. Her thighs trembled at the realization of what could happen here tonight. She knew immediately that she wanted it to happen, if he led she would follow. She turned to face him those soft brown eyes were only inches away.

Jeffrey's car crunched the gravel on his return, he entered the house calling, "Vanessa I'm home". Putting his things in the hall he called again. Nothing, this is odd he thought wondering where on Earth she could be. He toured the house before accepting the fact that she was not there. Slightly annoyed he made tea and proposed to wait for her return.

The sound of a car wakened him from a sleep, he looked at his watch, he had been home four hours, what was going on. He pushed at his glasses and was startled by the police car standing on the drive.

P.C. Johnson got out of the car, and said rather solemnly "Good morning Vicar".

Jeffrey rather mumbled his response, still a little dazed.

P.C. Johnson's face cracked into a smile and said "Look who I found struggling with all this shopping, had to give her lift didn't I". He opened the passenger door, and out stepped someone Jeffrey used to know.

"Vanessa"? Jeffrey said hesitatingly "Is that you ".

"Of course it is, don't you know your own wife Vicar " laughed the policeman, getting back into the car. "See you again Mrs Watkins".

"Yes, thanks again constable", she replied, turning to pick up her packages and walking into the house, pausing only to say "Hello Jeffrey".

"Vanessa what's happening, what's happened to you ", Jeffrey flapped, staring at this new apparition, "Your hair, your clothes, your......", his voice trailed away as he struggled to take in her new look.

"Jeffrey, I have merely done what most women do these days, had my hair cut and coloured, I am wearing make-up and I have bought some new clothes and shoes, that's all," she stated rather off-handedly.

"But you look, you look" he stammered to find the words.

"Younger and more confident, I think are the words you are looking for, at least according to P.C. Johnson." She smiled, and headed for the stairs.

"But, but why", whined Jeffrey following her.

"Because I am rejuvenating my soul Jeffrey, just like Saint Paul on the road to wherever it was". She raised a newly sculpted eyebrow trying to remember, but dropped it when she could not.

"Act...Actually it was Damascus, not that it's important, but what has brought about this ch.. change", Jeffrey stammered, standing in the bedroom door, finger to glasses.

She looked at him disapprovingly in the dressing-table mirror, whilst hanging the new clothes in the wardrobe.

"A postcard, and shaft of sunlight on a grey day", she smiled to herself,

"I am afraid that many things have to change Jeffrey. Firstly, I am going on holiday to California, when I return we will discuss the other changes".

"But what about me, what about the Parish ". Jeffrey's mood had changed from confusion to anger as he could already see the difficulties that lay ahead for him. "What if I refuse to let you go, refuse to accept this transformation". He took a step towards her. She stopped him with a look, through her new varilux contact lenses, and saw what a sad and weak man he had become.

"I will go anyway and never return", she stated flatly, and walked straight past him toward the stairs. Reaching the top she heard him cry.
"You couldn't not after all these years"
She turned to see him approaching her with his arms outstretched pleadingly. She took an involuntary step backward. The unaccustomed heels of her new shoes caught in the carpet, and with a scream she fell, tumbling and falling down the stairs into a silent, crumpled heap on the parquet flooring of the hall at the bottom. After the funeral, the Parish and the Bishop completely understood Jeffrey's wish to retire to a closed order of monks, and devote the rest of his life to meditation. He would never disclose the events that led up to the tragic accident.

Mrs Vanessa Watkins was buried beneath the Rhododendron bushes in the church graveyard. Jeffrey never discovered, or was even aware of the sender of the single, long stemmed rose that appeared the next and subsequent days.

THE INCIDENT AT THE BELGRAVE HOTEL

"Here we are at last." I said to my wife as our car crunched to a halt on the sandy coloured gravel of the forecourt to the Belgrave Hotel.

It seemed to have been a longer drive than usual to our favourite South Coast watering hole. The traffic had been heavy and the afternoon was losing its light. Not that it mattered really. In fact the anticipation of staying at the hotel again made the journey that much more bearable. We eased ourselves out of the car and stood for a moment looking at the place. The aching muscles in our not so young bodies needed some relief.

The Belgrave Hotel was a three story, stone built Victorian building, standing in its own small grounds. It stood on the corner of a road of similar if somewhat smaller properties three streets back from the sea front. A wall and a tall hedge of Copper Beeches surrounded the perimeter keeping it almost hidden from view, ensuring privacy. The stonework had darkened with pollution over the years'; allied to the rich dark mahogany woodwork it appeared rather severe. But at this time of the evening, gathering dusk, lights blazed from the three vertical bay windows and the open hall doorway, it reflected old world comfort and solidity.

"Mr. and Mrs. Jenkins welcome, welcome again, so nice to see you once more."

It was the "Wing Commander", officially known as Wing Commander Anthony Winstanley RAF (Rtd.). Sounded very stuffy when first we came, nothing could have been further from the truth. The man was politeness and affability personified, genuine too. His well- cut blazer with a wing crested badge on the breast pocket, regimental type striped tie confirmed his associations with the services. However he never fell into the tiresome trap of "Jolly good show," or "Wizard prang", mentality of some of his contemporaries.

The Winstanley family were mine hosts at the Belgrave, the Wing Commander as he was universally known, Gwen his wife, Robert their son and Susan their daughter-in-law. An excellent team they appeared to make, for the Hotel seemed to run like the proverbial Swiss watch, friendliness and service the watchwords.

"Mr. and Mrs. Shackleton arrived about an hour ago" the Wing Commander gushed walking us through the hall to the small reception desk, knowing we were about to ask whether our friends from Harrogate were in residence.

Reception seemed to be disappearing under a wealth of tourist literature. Brochures for every local park, garden, tour and entertainment festooned the well- lit area, situated below the sweeping, finely decorated wooden staircase.

"Must do our best to promote the facilities, keep the people coming to our little patch" beamed our host. His brown eyes twinkled above a thick moustache that must have been obligatory to grow when you joined the RAF, it was now however shot with silver to match his distinguished hairline. "Robert will park your car around the back, and bring your bags to your room, I'm sure you would like to freshen up".

We did. Our usual room was its normal warm comfortable self. A bunch of fresh Daffodils on the octagonal table in the bay window was the small personal touch that epitomizes the approach of the Winstanleys'. My wife emerging from the bathroom enveloped in a thick white toweling hotel robe commented.

"I wonder how they remember about the flowers, everybody has their local variety you know, Harry and Grace have White Roses".

"Yes" I replied "Probably all on computer now, as is knowing about our drinks at the bar, and the morning newspapers. Nice touches though."

We met our friends Harry and Grace Shackleton at dinner. The food was delicious, non-fancy wholesome cooking. Tables were set with immaculate white Irish linen cloths with stiff serviettes and embossed heavy cutlery. After a chat at the bar we all retired to bed, promising to catch up with all the gossip tomorrow, it had been a long day.

We were up and out early, this was only a weekend visit and we wanted to pack in as much as possible. A walk, arm in arm for mutual support along the promenade, we were well wrapped up against the keen wind coming off the sea. We could taste the salt on our lips from the spray blowing into our faces. Down to the Marina to gawp and wish at the expensive boats, then lunch at one of the pubs overlooking the harbour. A drive down the coast followed in the afternoon, returning to the Hotel in time for dinner. We settled in the bar later for a pleasant evening's conversation and reminiscences with our old friends.

The time was passing pleasantly. It was about ten o'clock when I saw a man and a woman entering the bar, they were strangers to me, and I assumed they were new guests. I happened to be at the bar ordering drinks from the Wing Commander who had been in top form all evening. I saw him stiffen at the sight of these people, and he suddenly lost all of his "bon-homie".

"What do you want here ?". He snapped angrily at the man, who slumped on to a bar stool, he had obviously been drinking somewhere else previously.

I looked at the man out of the corner of my eye as I stood at the bar. He was in his mid-forties overweight and pasty faced, greasy dark hair fell over his face. His shirt buttons were performing miracles keeping his stomach contained within the material. A beige creased linen suit completed an unsavoury looking character

The woman, a small mousey creature appeared extremely

embarrassed to be here, looking furtively about, almost as if trying to find somewhere to hide.

"Surely you wouldn't deny me a drink, on this my birthday, or had you forgotten ?", slurred the man.

"One drink then you'll have to leave, wait just a minute", the Wing Commander turned to me "Sorry Mr. Jenkins, your drinks coming up", he turned to pull them.

"O.K. Wing Commander no problem", I said looking nowhere in particular.

"Wing Commander ? Hah !" Exclaimed the fat man, "Don't tell me he's got you believing that old chestnut, has he ?", he snorted loudly, turning his sweating face toward me. "I think Leading Aircraftsman is nearer the mark, doesn't sound so snooty though does it, eh" he sneered sarcastically.

"I've no idea what you are talking about", I ventured adopting a patronising air.

"Ask him then, go on ask him", the man persisted leaning further toward me his supporting forearm sliding down the bar. "And while you're at it, ask him who I am". Without waiting for an answer he continued "I'm only his bloody son that's all, his first born, but does he acknowledge me does he Hell". He virtually shouted that last remark.

I looked at the Wing Commander, he seemed to be crumbling, his shoulders sank, his head bowed. The louder the man spoke, the smaller he seemed to become. The conversation in the bar had stopped, everyone was looking at him. The silence seemed to encourage the drunk. He had an audience and he was going to play to it.

"Let's ask him another question shall we ?", boomed the apparent son turning uncertainly on the bar stool. "Let's ask him why he threw my mother and me out of this place, and took up with the woman he now calls his wife, and her Bastard son ?".

The atmosphere in the room was now stiff with embarrassment. The Wing Commander looked like a balloon with a slow leak. This drunken tirade was having its effect. People were leaving the bar.

"Don't go, don't go yet he hasn't answered the questions", the drunk said belligerently.

"Gordon, I've had enough let's go", his companion pulled at his sleeve, he slapped her hand away.

"Not until he answers the questions for his guests". He swung his arm in a faltering arc as if to identify everyone. The word guests, was spat out.

"He might not answer them, but I will".

A firm voice from the doorway, it was Robert. He walked into the room, stopped and glared at the intruder.
Robert was not the largest of men, slightly above average height and of medium build, but he seemed to grow larger as he walked further into the room. His right forefinger pointed accusingly.

"Your Mother was a drunken slut, and you a thief and a loudmouth. Between you both, you would have ruined all the work he put into the Hotel. He had also divorced your Mother before he met mine. There's your answers. Now are you going or am I going to throw you out."

Robert's tone was final and threatening. He took two or three steps towards the other man putting him within reach.

The woman tugged at the drunk's open jacket.

"Gordon let's go now, we don't want any trouble here".

She knew, and the drunken man should have known that he would be no match for Robert who was younger, fitter and more determined. However the alcohol obviously clouded the man's judgment for with a drunken growl he threw an off balance punch at Robert. Robert quickly side stepped the punch and moved forward slapping the man's face twice, forehand and backhand. The sound of the slaps cracked across the room and the man staggered backward against the bar. Without its support he would have undoubtedly fallen to the floor.

The valiant shirt buttons gave up the struggle and four popped off, his shirt gaped open and his stomach protruded somehow encapsulating this sorry figure, his face reddening by the second.

Robert moved once again but this time only to grab the man by the jacket collar, frog marching him out and threw him onto the forecourt gravel near his car. The woman wailed and sobbed.

"Go and don't ever come back, for I'll be here waiting", warned Robert.

The woman literally pushed the drunk into the passenger seat slamming the door, rushing around to the driver's side got in. The car skidded on the gravel as it shot off.

The whole incident had lasted no more than twelve to fifteen minutes, yet it seemed like an hour. I still stood by the bar in amazement. I looked at Robert's recent growth in stature. Perhaps he had been content to be a team member at the hotel, always available but never at the forefront leaving that to his father, subsequently never really being noticed. He had suddenly taken centre stage and the spotlight was on him.

He looked quickly behind the bar. The Wing Commander had disappeared. Robert looked at me, I smiled reassuringly, he walked to the centre of the room.

"Ladies and Gentlemen, may I on behalf of the family and the Hotel apologise for the intrusion into your evening. I fully understand if you wish to retire to your rooms, if not the drinks for the rest of the evening will be at the Hotel's expense". He returned to his place behind the bar. "Now then Mr. Jenkins can I finish serving your round ?".

Then a strange thing happened. People applauded. A sustained round of applause greeted Robert who was surprised and somewhat embarrassed.

However no-one retired and the previously subdued atmosphere lightened considerably and everyone's heads were much closer during their conversations. The Wing Commander did not re-appear.

He did near the end of breakfast time the next morning, supported by the rest of his family. They stood together at the table which held the large selection of cereals and fruit juices. The Wing Commander seemed to have recovered much of his composure, but was not quite the man he had been. He was wearing a plain cardigan and no tie.

"Ladies and Gentlemen", he began a little nervously, "May I on behalf of my family attempt to explain last night's happening, as an apology for the intrusion into your stay here at the Belgrave. I can say that………".

Ex Police Inspector Harry Shackleton rose from our table and stopped him mid-sentence.

"Wing Commander", Harry heavily emphasized the title, "Neither you nor your family have any need to explain the ramblings of a drunken non-resident", again heavily emphasized, "I know I speak on behalf of all your guests, when I say that The Belgrave Hotel has provided us with many excellent holidays in the past due to your professionalism and friendliness. We see no reason why that should not continue into the future. Last evening is already forgotten".

Harry sat down to small round of applause and mutterings of "Hear, Hear", from around the room.

Checking out was emotional, full of warm handshakes and moist eyeson behalf of the Winstanleys. Harry and I had booked our next visit in a few months as had most of the guests, as a gesture of solidarity.

The Wing Commander fully restored in his blazer and tie bade us a safe journey and assured us of a warm welcome on our return. Robert now was at his side.

The town was disappearing in the rear view mirror, when my wife mused.

"I wonder if he really was ? ………..

"Annie", I said "We all agreed not to, didn't we." She sighed resignedly.

It was intriguing though.

CHRISTMAS CRACKERS

I looked again. He was still there. Standing in the doorway of an empty shop with windows that still said "Closing Down Sale, Everything Must Go". Everything had gone.

The disadvantaged in this city, of which he appeared to be one, used the doorway itself as a sometime dormitory. The man was dressed like a down and out. An old brown coat tied with an odd coloured belt, a multi-coloured scarf knotted around his neck and tucked inside the coat. Frayed trousers holed at the knee, aand battered shoes with string for laces. His hair was long, greying and thin, the wind blowing it in swirls around his head. Shaving was obviously not a daily routine, yet his blue eyes shone like dark sapphires

What caught my attention was that this picture of human misery was not begging but selling. They were Christmas Crackers, quite obviously home-made. He must at some time have seen Blue Peter for they appeared to be toilet rolls covered with Christmas wrapping paper, just like a child would make.

The fact that this was the middle of June either hadn't occurred to him, or he didn't care. No-one else seemed to care either for in the couple of hours since I first noticed him he hadn't appeared to have sold any of his wares. The whole picture looked so bizarre that in the end I couldn't resist it and I walked over.

"Hello" he said as I approached, his face wrinkling in a whiskery warm smile like a friendly hedgehog, "Would you like to buy a Cracker".?

"How much are they"? I asked warily, "Isn't a bit odd selling Christmas Crackers in June, it's somewhat out of season", I ventured, looking down at the small assortment of colours arranged on an upturned cardboard box.

"The Christmas spirit should never be out of season, and if you can find love and understanding in your heart it can be Christmas all year round. Go on buy a Cracker or two" he cajoled, shuffling them with his dirty-nailed hands.

"Buy one for your partner too, I promise you won't be sorry". His eyes were almost incandescently bright now. I could hardly look away. How did he know I had a partner.

"Show me the money in your right hand pocket" the man said confidently. I did as I was told and opened my hand.

"There we are, just right" he said gleefully plucking a Five Pound note out of my palm with his thumb and forefinger, like a bird taking a worm from the ground.

"Which do you prefer"? he asked, and before I could make any kind of protest, "It doesn't really matter as it is you that will make the difference".

I chose two quickly, and walked away feeling more than a little foolish. Through my own curiosity I had been conned by a psychic tramp. I looked at the pathetic bundles for which I had just paid Five Pounds. Something was rattling around inside; them perhaps this would not be a complete loss after all. Before turning into the car park I looked back to see if anyone else had been as inquisitive as I had been, but the man had gone. I returned to my car thinking my Five Pounds was already being swallowed in the nearest Pub.

Julie and I had been going through a sustained rough patch of late; it was simply the pressure of life. I had to take on an advance computer course to maintain my position at work. This meant long nights in front of the monitor and little conversation. She too had to work odd hours at the hospital and we were going days without seeing one another.

I had also recently had a blazing row with my brother about the fact that I was not visiting our ageing parents enough.

How the Hell could I.? I physically could not fit it all in.

However Julie had made me promise that Saturday night we would have a meal together and talk things out. I thought the Crackers might bring a little light relief.

We were having coffee after our meal when I brought out the Crackers and showed them to Julie. I explained how I had got them. She laughed out loud, her long dark hair fell about her face. It reminded me of how beautiful I thought she was.

"He must have really seen you coming" her big brown eyes gleaming and re-enforcing my opinion of her. But she took a Cracker and shook it, the rattle demanded investigation.

"Let's pull them together like at Christmas" I suggested. We did. The Crackers were having the desired effect we were becoming our old selves again. Softening and relaxing, re-discovering each other.

The Crackers broke open easily. In each was a small, circular mirror about two and half inches in diameter encased in white plastic with a handle. A child's looking glass. Julie and I glanced at each other amusingly as we held the mirrors up close and looked into them.

At first only my own reflection was visible. Then as I looked closer the image changed. I could only gasp as my family was revealed sitting around the dining table at home at Christmas time. There were my parents laughing and happy just as I remembered them.

Father was in an oversize jumper knitted by an aunt. Mother was in a floral pinny and a paper hat. My brother and I, we no more than nine or ten years' old, also wearing coloured hats and shining faces. Decorations adorned the room with presents and wrapping paper scattered about under a large Christmas tree. I was suddenly filled with that special feeling you have at Christmas when you are young. I had to swallow hard at the lump that formed in my throat brought on by the treasured memories of those happy times. I tore my eyes away, I wanted to tell Julie what I was seeing, but she was staring just as intently at her mirror with tears running down her lovely cheeks feeling exactly the same emotions, watching her family at a past Christmas.

She looked up and tenderly held out her hand. We held each other very tightly both overcome with the special warmth that had radiated from the mirrors. Love and understanding had returned to us, by way of Christmas Crackers in the middle of June.

Just who was that old man!

Sunlight, warmth and positivity had re-entered my life replacing the cold grey clouds of frustration. Tomorrow I would ring my brother.

THE MESSAGE ON THE WALL

"Rob, answer that bloody telephone, if it's the Inspector looking for me I'm out chasing a lead, if it's the press we don't know anything yet, if it's my wife I'll be home late, and if it's God I'm not ready to go just yet", Rob smiled a patronising smile at my attempted humour and picked up the receiver. It was option one.

"Inspector Roberts, said to contact him on your return", Rob said smugly, as if putting one over on me for making him lie to a superior officer.

Detective Constable Lane was ambitious, and lying to Detective Inspectors was in his view planting seed on stony ground. I did not care. Things were busy enough normally, but what with my regular D.C. retiring, and having a younger ladder climber foisted on me, the burglaries had started.

Ordinarily burglary is a nuisance crime. However when they are cleverly done, leave very few clues, are clearly profitable, and happen to pillars of the community then burglary becomes an issue.

Steal a Radio through an open kitchen window it's a statistic, steal some Silverware or Antique Collectable from the large detached in its own grounds and the Vikings have landed. Well they had landed, and |I have been handed the task of preventing rape and pillage by rounding them up and explaining the errors of their ways.

Me that is Det. Sgt. David Blake husband and father of this parish, at your service, through all the unsociable hours, and associating with all the unsociable people, whilst you, the public sleep soundly in your beds. Unfortunately, not all are sleeping, some are complaining loudly at some length to the local press, to my superiors, and they all appear to be dialling my telephone number.

"Don't forget you are coming over to dinner tonight, Sarge," called Rob.

"As if I would", I called back, actually I had forgotten, and waited for him to go out of the room, before ringing my wife,

"It's all right, I've remembered, and everything's organised, just be home on time for a change", she said warningly.

Later as we drew up outside Rob's house my wife said "Why didn't we start our married life with a three bedroom detached house, with garage on a new estate",

Thinking quickly, and answering truly, "Because you, somehow were with child, and your father had not been in business, nor was he successful enough to give us a deposit on such a house Darling", I replied sweetly receiving a dig in the ribs for my cheek.

Rob answered the door bell, and welcomed us in. His wife entered the hall from the lounge,

"This is Marion my wife", said Rob, and we did the mutual introductions.

Now I am a happily married man, and I love my wife, but I could not prevent myself from staring at this perfectly entrancing young woman. She was of medium height, pencil slim, elegant build, with long dark shining hair simply cut with a fringe down to her arched eyebrows. It seemed to frame her face perfectly, and accentuated the palest, and most mesmeric green eyes I have ever seen. Her movements were controlled and specific, if she had flown about the room, I would not have been surprised. The meal was excellent, the evening convivial, and it flashed by.

On the way home my wife said "You had better watch your step, there's a young man on his way up, whether he wants to or not, and he had better want to or else. That young lady is used to, and expects success. Did you take your eyes off her for long enough to look at the room, no I don't suppose you did. It was gorgeous, Daddy must be very generous". She sat back with an air of satisfaction having told me a thing or two.

I mumbled something about, of course I had seen the room, and reminded her that they are both working, and had good jobs, but really all I could see were those pale green eyes, and we both knew it.

Two days later, events took a rather sinister twist. Street patrols had been stepped up, due to the robberies, and during an early morning check to the rear of business properties, a body was found in a lane. By the time we arrived, the premises fronting the lane, a silversmith and high class gift shop had been found to be entered and robbed.

"Do we know who the body is yet", I asked Rob, who had been closer than I when the call came, and had arrived first.

"Yes, the beat bobby knew her straight away, its Annie the Alkie". He stated.

The scene of the crime was taped off, we ducked under the tape, and I knelt to look at the body.

"It's a bit of a mess Sarge", Rob said gently, making a statement rather than asking a question, and it was.

Her clothes, such as they were, for she was always dressed in whatever she could find, were ripped to shreds in some places, and were blood-soaked. She must have had twenty or thirty stab wounds to her front and back.

"I cannot remember such a frenzied attack, whoever did it must have gone completely mad", I said thinking aloud "She must have surprised the burglars, and they have made absolutely sure she would not live to tell the tale".

Poor Annie I thought, completely harmless, if a bloody nuisance due to her addictions. Most local coppers knew her she had been picked so many times for drunkenness, and prostitution over the years. Funnily enough though, during her brief periods of lucidity, she was an intelligent woman, with quite a good education. However, married the wrong bloke, a drunk, stood on the slippery slope, and slipped ever downward. There was a teenage son somewhere, I seemed to remember, but whatever she was she did not deserve to die like this.

"What's that on the wall Sarge," asked Rob pointing.

I looked following his finger. The body was in a crumpled heap facing the whitened block wall. The wall itself was spattered with splashes of blood, but near the base were marks that could be letters. I knelt again it was hard to decipher, but it looked like the letters CREEP followed by a dash, or an "I", but it could have been a splash mark.

"Make sure that we get that photographed, and get the forensic boys to check her fingers Rob", I said sharply, this event was getting to me, "and I also want a precise time of death, this is the first mistake our burglars have made, if that's a message I want to make sure it's not in vain". I left the scene of one crime to look at the scene of another.

The account of the robbery was all too familiar. Alarms expertly silenced the minimum of damage only to effect entry and exit. No fingerprints or clues of any kind, and only small expensive pieces taken. The impression given was of speed and efficiency, a professional job. However the murder had been completely the opposite clumsy and messy, amateur. It was as if two separate people were involved, which might be the case I had no idea how many this gang might contain.

There was no point to my staying at the scene, I would receive the reports from the officers involved and study them later. I called to Rob and we returned to the office where I knew telephones would be glowing red by now, and my superiors would be more than a little keen to hear of what progress I was making. My replies were becoming ever more diplomatic, as I was not making any progress, it was too soon.

After having fed the baying hounds of the media, with some bland facts and standard responses, fenced off Inspector Roberts with a spurious report of new evidence, which I was absolutely sure would lead somewhere and secure an arrest, Rob and I had an opportunity to review this latest crime

The robbery was now incidental, all our concentrations had to now centre on the murder, which if we could crack it would also put a stop to the other activities. We were pouring carefully over the preliminary photographs of the scene, and in particular the word, or part of a word, written by Annie on the wall. I was looking at it through a large magnifying glass, when I caught Rob smiling at me.

"Where's the pipe and deerstalker Sherlock" ? He laughed.

If he was expecting the classic clichéd response, he didn't get it. I disregarded his attempted humour, I had too much on my mind.

"Look at this word on the wall", I said pointedly "C.R.E.E.P.", spelling out the letters, "There's no mistaking that is there, the only bone of contention, is that mark after the P, part of another letter or not," Rob looked, but it was impossible to tell, there were too many blood splashes surrounding it. I stood up and reached for my jacket.

"Come on, let's go" I said. "Before you ask, Annie tried to tell us something, to discover what that is we have to find out more about Annie, and quickly. We are going to her home, you had better check her address", I spoke the last words over my shoulder as I went out the door, leaving him to scramble through the paperwork, grab his coat and run after me to the car. I'll give him Sherlock.

The fact that Annie had anywhere to live at all would have been a surprise to anyone who came into contact with her she looked like the original bag lady. She had inherited a small terrace house from an aunt who had not seen her for many years and must have still had a picture of her as a child. The adult Annie would have inherited nothing.

We drew up across the street. Walking up to the front door I thought that this house at some time must have been reasonable premises. There was no point in knocking on the front door as it was swaying gently back and forth in the gusty wind. The interior of the house was a predictable stench laden chaos of rubbish and terminal decline. The remaining furniture, what there was of it, must have been like the decor, original to the house.

"Do you mean to tell me that we have to search this, this place", said Rob, his descriptive powers failing him, in his search for a suitable place name.

"I'm afraid so", I said, sharing his disgust at the thought. "First and foremost though, I think we had better see if there is any one at home". Rob looked at me in amazement, it had not struck him that anyone else could or would live in these conditions. "She is married, and has at least one child of teenage years," I said quoting her file.

We shouted from the passageway, there was no reply and we made our way through the three downstairs rooms trying not to touch anything. This was not for any forensic or scene of crime reasons, it was plain and simple revulsion.

Rob turned at the bottom of the stairs and said "I am not going any further without gloves or some protective clothing my wife would not let me back in the house in these clothes if she knew."

The image of his wife and those beautiful green eyes seemed like a Champagne cascade to a man in the desert as we stood in that narrow disgusting passageway.

"You are probably right, neither would mine," I said, not quite as convincingly.

"We do have overalls and gloves in the boot of the car", he said, and marched off to get them, without waiting for my O.K.

I radioed for some assistance in our search and explained the hazards, whilst we put on our overalls. We returned across the street looking as if we were about to inspect the drains, which was not too far from the truth.

We started up the stairs and I called out once more. Still no reply although there was a sound. The sound was snoring. As we entered the bedroom at the top of the stairs, a man lay diagonally across a mound of clothes lost to the world. I shook him, but the smell of his breath told me that it would take some time to for him to come to, I decided to work around him.

The bedroom held nothing but clothes, empty bottles, and assorted rubbish.

"Rob check that room," I said pointing to the second bedroom, "I'll look in the front", I pushed at the front bedroom door, it held. I pushed harder it held firm, it was locked. Surprised, I summoned Rob.

"We can't break it down, we don't have a warrant", he said.
I agreed, and kicked the door until it splintered open. I was an impatient man on a mission today, and in the surroundings the door did not look out of place.

Our mouths fell open as we entered that room. It was in comparison to the rest of the house, pristine. In an ordinary home it would be pretty tidy, but here, well it was a shock. The bed was made and covered in a Liverpool F.C. Duvet. The wardrobe was full of designer label young man's clothes. It had a stand containing remote control television, sound system, and computer, all top of the range models. This was a young man with plenty of spare cash that he did not get from his parents.

"I can see why there is a lock on this door," I said. A shout from below, it was the local bobbies I had requested to help.

"First job, wake him up", I said pointing to sleeping beauty, "I want to know whose room that is, and as much as we can about him. I'll be downstairs".

I won't go into detail about the search downstairs. Just imagine the problem of rotting food, numerous animals and a rodent population couple that to human beings whose all-consuming and only thought was where the next drink was coming from. I eventually came upon an alcove cupboard in which among many other things, was an old square tin that had once contained a Christmas selection of biscuits. It now contained two photographs, and a few papers. One photograph was of a baby, the other was of a young girl in her school uniform. The papers were a birth certificate, a school report and assorted bills.

"Rob let's go, I think I've found all that we are going to find. We need to talk to him", I said pointing to the drunk, "Tell them to bring him to the office, and secure this house front and back. I also want a watch put on this place, in case our young entrepreneur returns".

Back at the Police Station, the interview with the drunken man was brief. The main reason being his brain was so addled with drink he could hardly tell day from night, and so the answers to anything more difficult than that would have been impossible to rely on. The other reason, which ran the first one a very close second, was that he stank to high heaven, this in the close proximity of an interview room made it unbearable. We returned him into the caring hands of the local Social Services Department.

It was late. I was tired, but I felt that mythical feeling that I was on the right track, but to where I did not know. I rang my wife to tell her I would be home later. She knew better than to ask what time, we had had this conversation too many times before. I asked Rob had he contacted his wife. My conscience was faintly nagging, only faintly, but I was conscious of the relatively short length of time they had been together.

I need not have worried she was apparently staying over-night in Dublin, on business with her Managing Director, a female Rob hastened to add. I enquired abstractedly if she enjoyed her job. Rob replied that he thought so, but that the consistent pressure and continual travel, both within this country and abroad, was wearing at times, but that was the nature of her job, as Personal Assistant to the M.D.

His answer was intriguing. Was all not hunky dory at the Lane household, perhaps the entrancing Marion was more interested in her job, than her husband. I resolved to retell this story, to she who can interpret the hieroglyphics of all life as we know it, when I got home.

I resumed reading the reports from the beat constable and his door to door enquiries along the street, about the people who lived in the house we had visited today. I was most interested in the teenager and his activities. The only information available was that he stayed at the house frequently, but generally only overnight, which was one night longer than I would have stayed. It was rumoured that he also shared a flat with another lad somewhere in town, but where no-one knew. It was imperative that we find it.

I heard the telephone ringing from far away in another land where everything was soft and warm, and I tried to ignore it. My wife did not let me.

"Wake up its Alan on his mobile, and he says it's urgent", she said pushing me.

Alan was the officer on night watch at the house.

"Sarge," he said softly "Someone is trying to break into the house, I think it's the boy you want to question, shall I arrest him".
I was immediately awake, and looked at the bedside clock, it was 2.30 am.

"No, I don't think he will get in without making a noise as we have changed the locks and he won't be prepared for it. When he realises what's happened, he will go back to town. Try and follow him. I am on my way. Keep in touch with where you are, and I'll come to you. Don't lose him". I ordered.

The boy was clever he had parked a car two streets away. Alan had to follow him on foot from the house. When the boy drove away Alan was stranded, but he did note the licence number.

"I'm sorry Sarge" Alan's apologies came breathlessly over the mobile phone. I was still en route. "By the time I had got back to my car, he could have gone anywhere".

I braked. Pulling in to the side of the road, "O.K. Alan", I said frustration putting an edge to my voice, "But, did he see you ?".

Alan's reply was firm "No, I am certain he did not see me",.

I tapped the steering wheel with my fingers, "Good, this might not be such a dead loss after all. Radio that licence number and vehicle description to headquarters. I want a name and address of that car's owner as soon as I get to the station. Tell them I'm on my way in."

The uniformed desk Sergeant handed me the note as I walked in, "Evening Dave, heard this was a rush job, I've asked records to check whether it's on the reported as stolen lists, won't be long".

I muttered my thanks and looked at the name and address as I walked to the office. Knowing deep down that it would be a stolen car, this boy was smart, but there had been just a chance. However the address proved it, the car was from outside the town. A telephone call from records confirmed it, reported stolen three days ago.

I sat and drank a second, or was it a third cup of coffee. It was probable that the boy would only keep a stolen car for a short time then dump it, and steal another. Was three days too short a time. He might keep it a few days longer, he was not, as far as I knew, aware that we were onto him. I rang the desk Sergeant and told him to circulate the vehicle's number and description to all beat bobbies and traffic patrols. I want a search of the town at first light, if found just report its location, and keep a very low key observation. It was an outside chance but I deserved it.

A knock on the door roused me and I cursed myself, I had fallen asleep at my desk.

"Thought you might like a cup of tea Sarge", I looked up to see Rob bearing down on me with a steaming mug. This made me feel worse, he had caught me sleeping, I was supposed to be the experienced officer done it all, hard as nails, superman, and all that crap. He looked fresh and alive. I felt like a Guy Fawkes dummy ready for the fire.

"Why didn't you call me", he asked "I could have saved you all that", referring to last night, by the sweeping motion of his hand, over me and the desk.

Patronising young sod I thought, but would you have done what I had done, I said nothing. "Are you up to speed with the events", I eventually asked, after allowing the tea to part humanise me. He

was. The Sergeant on the front desk had told him as he was going off duty and Rob was coming in. "You are early any way aren't you", I enquired curiously.

"Yes", he admitted, "My wife returned on an earlier flight than expected. The M.D. wanted to get an early start in the office some new deal or other. She came in about Six and said she would crash out for an hour, so I came in". He looked a little crestfallen, it had not been his enthusiasm for the job that had allowed him to catch me off guard then, extra hieroglyphs for the great translator here I thought.

"Right lads", I addressed the small team of C.I.D. officers at my disposal, "I am going home to freshen up. I am then going to follow up on the photographs we found at the house. Rob you check on the birth certificate, the rest of you stay alert. Go out and search for this car, if we do get lucky, stake it out, and follow anyone who goes near it. We have to find that house or flat, or wherever it is he lives, keep in touch".

St. Agnes Grammar School for Girls it said on the photograph, and on the gymslip badge of the teenage, blonde girl in the frame. St. Agnes's had changed from a Grammar School into a small Comprehensive, and the girl in the photograph had, I suspected changed into Annie the Alkie. Using the mobile phone I rang ahead, to ask the Head Teacher for half an hour of his or her time. It was a her. According to the secretary unfortunately the Head was away, but the Deputy Head would see me, she was a her as well.

"Thank you for seeing me at such short notice", I commenced politely, "I was hoping you might be able to help me with some information, about a former pupil".

"If I can I will", she responded openly. The Deputy Head was a

woman in her mid Fifties, pleasant enough to look at, starting to thicken at the hips, and grey wisps in her dark hair.

"This is the girl I am interested in, her name is Anne Mcgovern, and she would have been a pupil here during...", the Deputy Head cut me off.

"I remember Anne", she said, "I was Head Girl here then, and this was a tragic case. Anne became pregnant when she was Seventeen. She was expelled from this school, which was a different place in those days, a Grammar School for Girls, and very straight laced with it. Her mother died from a heart attack, for which her father blamed Anne, due to the shock and the shame of the pregnancy. After the expulsion from school, he sent her off to a relation in London, we never saw her again." She looked back at the photograph.

I filled in the rest of Annie's life as I knew it, and her sad demise. Tears moistened the eyes of the woman across the desk, "That is an extremely sad story, for someone I remember quite well as a happy, intelligent girl, who enjoyed most aspects of school life, particularly school plays and musical groups", an inspirational thought struck her, " Do you know I think there are still some photographs of them here, have you a minute whilst I find them".

I smiled appreciatively. She rose and went out of the room, and returned ten minutes later with several leather bound albums, leafing through them and stopping when the pages she was searching for arrived. Smilingly she turned the albums for me to see, leaning over the desk to point to Annie in a large group of girls all dressed in costume for some show or other. The photograph was in black and white, but the one underneath, a smaller group, which represented girls taking part from each age group, was in colour.

Annie was at the centre, smiling broadly, with five other girls of differing, younger ages, surrounding her. It was a poignant picture, possibly the last time she had been at the centre of admiration and happiness. I gazed at it, her fall from teenage innocence had been rapid, culminating in a terrible fashion. I handed the album back sadly, thanked the teacher, and made my exit.

Driving back to town in sober mood, the image of that photograph stayed in my mind. The mobile rang, bringing me back to the pressing tasks in hand.

"We've found it, we've found it, and we have it staked out", shouted Alan excitedly, he gave me the location.

"Excellent, I am on my way, don't make any moves unless you have to, " I said catching the excitement, but something else was ringing a bell in the back of my head, it would have to wait.

Annie's death had been the catalyst in this case, the burglaries had continued for months without so much as a clue, but now only three days since her body had been discovered I felt the initiative had passed to us, and we were close. I parked my car some distance away from the location Alan had given me, and started walking in that direction.

I saw Rob waiting outside the newsagent's shop as arranged. The car was located behind a group of shops, in an area which served as parking for tenants in blocks of flats. They were five storeys high, and overlooked the car park on three sides.

Rob explained how the car had been found, by an off duty traffic policeman visiting his grandparents who lived in one of the ground floor apartments. This was a double dose of luck, for we could now observe the car without arousing suspicion. The only question was, had the car been dumped here, or was this the living quarters of our quarry.

At the precise moment that thought went through my mind, Rob's radio started to speak. "There are two suspects leaving the flats, heading in the general direction of the car park, are you able to observe, over", the officer in the flat was reporting.

It was Rob's turn, "Alan can you see them", he had placed Alan who was the only one to have seen the boy, in an unmarked car as close as he could, but armed Alan with a long zoom lens camera.

Alan's voice came back "The one boy has the same outfit on, as last time. Same baseball cap, Jacket with the same logos, and the same pattern trainers, don't know about the other, he's dressed similarly but with different logos, and he has dark glasses on." Alan was keeping his voice as low, and as calm as possible, "They are splitting up. Our boy is heading for the car, the other lad toward another vehicle, what do you want to do". His voice was anxious and questioning.

I had to make a decision and quickly, I decided not to stretch our luck, if we lost them now, who knows, "This is Sergeant Blake", I said snatching Rob's radio "Everyone move in now, let's take them. Alan, try and block one exit with your car, move ", I shouted the instructions as Rob and I ran down the block of shops around the corner and into the car park.

The two boys were still walking towards their separate vehicles, when Alan's car screeched to a stop, they looked up and saw us all running. I shouted "Stop, police". Completely pointless of course, but I had followed procedure. The two boys tried to get to their cars the stolen Escort and our boy were closer to Rob and me. We made for them. Alan and the others were slightly further away from the

other lad, he was able to reach his car. Smoke and screams came from the rear tyres as it shot backwards, narrowly missing the officer running from his grandparents flat. More smoke and even noisier screams came from the front tyres as it tore forward.

Alan to his everlasting credit stood his ground at the exit with his arm raised, until the very last moment and would have been killed had he not thrown himself to one side. The escaping car smashed into the rear quarter of Alan's vehicle forcing it out of the way, and raced away down the road.

All this happened in my peripheral vision as I ran hard to prevent the same thing happening to us. Rob and I reached the car just as the boy was slamming the door. I wrenched it open and grabbed for the boys hand as he was trying to turn the key to start the engine. Rob came in from the other side and we had him.

As soon as I was sure he was secure I raced off to see if Alan was all right. Thankfully he was. He was dusting himself down, and looking a little sheepish "Sorry, Sarge I couldn't stop it", he said, I assured him he had done all he could, and I would mention his bravery to our superiors.

"Did you get the number Alan", I said quickly. I was sure he would have done, he had had a close up view of it. He said that he'd got it, and the vehicle type, it was one of those sporty little hatchback jobs, very quick off the mark they are. "Get the details on the radio, stop and arrest this time", I told him, "And tell them I want to know who that car is registered to and the address as soon as they can. Rob and I will wait here just in case this is it", I said waving my arm in the general direction of the flats.

Our suspect was taken back to the station, whilst Rob and I waited. Two minutes we waited not bad going for headquarters. This indeed

was it. The car was registered to a Mr. Martin Lake at an address here in the flats.

We found it. It was as anonymous as the rest, nothing singled it out. Paintwork was shiny and neat, net curtains looked clean, no litter. Mr. & Mrs Average could live here, but they did not. Two teenage tearaways that we knew of, lived here possibly more, the facts did not come together. We would have to wait for a warrant to enter this premises that could take until tomorrow.

I could not wait, the best I could hold our suspect on was car theft I had to have something else to keep him in custody. "Rob get me Inspector Roberts on the phone", he knew what I was going to do. Roberts had the power to allow me to enter the flat, and sort the warrant out later. I explained the situation, and loaded it with references to evidence with which to crack the case, early arrest, something for the press, taking the pressure of us all, that sort of thing.

"You should have gone to bloody R.A.D.A., with a performance like that", Rob said, shaking his head in disbelief as we forced the front door.

"He wants a result as badly as we do", I replied, stating the truth.

The flat was as well-equipped and fitted as the boys bedroom, only more so. Everything was top quality, and well designed. We moved from room to room, it was spick and span, and faintly familiar. I put it down to a Department Store layout my wife must have dragged me to at some time.

"O.K., O.K.", I said "We are impressed, but let's look for something that might justify my request to Inspector Roberts".

Absolutely nothing incriminating, it appeared to be a luxury flat and nothing else. I sat dejected, we were going to take away some paperwork, bank statements and the like that might lead somewhere, but no hard evidence.

As a last resort I said "Photograph the ornaments, the pictures, the plates everything, something might be on our list of stolen property. Get them developed and blown up, as soon as possible, we will circulate them to the burglary victims, someone might recognise an item," I was desperate.

Driving back to the police station, I tried to gather my thoughts. Ran the facts of the case through the mental sorting process, but frustration and depression prevented logic from prevailing. I needed a diversion, the way when you cannot find something, look for another item quite unrelated and invariably your original object will appear. I had told Rob to initially interview our suspect, Alan was on the paper trail. I decided to answer the school bell still ringing at the back of my head.

The Deputy Head had the photographs I had asked for over the telephone open and ready on her desk when I arrived.

"What is it you are looking for", she asked enquiringly.

"I am not sure, but there is something in my head", I replied without looking up, concentrating on the images. I came back to the snap of Annie surrounded by younger girls, and my eyes drew me to the smallest figure. This was it. The young face stared out broodingly. It was unsmiling, there was no joy or youthful excitement at being chosen for this photograph as with the others, even Annie looked radiant. Yet, this face was familiar.

"Do you know who this girl is", I asked almost casually, turning the album around to face the teacher. She looked hard and long, but negatively.

"No, I cannot say that I do but I can find her name, and that might help". With that she took the photograph from its mounts on the page, and turned it over. Running her finger down the back, there was a list of the students' names. She stopped on M. Crawley, and sat back in her chair, looking out through the arched windows.

 "Something, something", she said hesitatingly, and reached for the telephone, dialling an internal number. "Oh John, is Joanne there please", she said, and then covering the mouthpiece with her other hand, she whispered to me "The Staff room, Joanne is another old girl of the school, a little younger than me, she might remember", she broke off "Joanne, Hello, its Margaret here, I wonder if you can help", and proceeded to name the girl, giving her school dates, and a description from the photograph. "Yes, Oh yes, Marion Crawley, I remember now that has to be her doesn't it, I had left then, but I recall the tales now, thank you Jo", she replaced the receiver, and looked at me.

"I did not know this girl personally, you understand," she said seriously "but I have heard stories about here from former pupils", she looked out of the window again, "She was apparently a very spoiled young lady, always wanted to be at the centre of attention, you know the type, and would do anything to achieve it. Sneak to teachers, betray friendships, anything. Ultimately she became known throughout the school as "Creepy Crawley", one of those adolescent nick names that apparently was adopted even by the teachers whilst she was here".

At the sound of the prefix, I shot upright in my chair, and did my pointer dog impression. Suddenly my mind was crystal clear. "Does

anyone know what happened to her", I shot the question at the teacher.

"Not really", she said surprised by the anxiousness in my voice "She did not finish her academic time here, her father moved his business to another part of the country, I understand she left just before her last year". She sat back, and crossed her hands in her tartan skirted lap, justifiably proud that she had been able to answer my questions about a pupil long since departed from the school. She was not aware of course of the implications of her answers, or the effects on the lives of the people concerned. She had simply pushed the first domino.

I firstly, had to be certain that Marion Lane's maiden name had been Crawley that would not be difficult to check, in my heart I knew already.

Creepy Crawley, it was juvenile, the sort of nickname that might have come from Enid Blyton's pen, but there was nothing childlike about the owner of the name now. She was a murderer, and a clever thief. I now knew who she was, but I would have a hell of a time proving it without some absolutely cast iron proof. The fact that she was married to my Detective Constable was going to make for some extremely delicate investigations on my part.

The beautiful colouring of her eyes was now, obviously, down to coloured contact lenses, for the young girl in the photograph had brown eyes, and that is what had thrown me at first, the rest of her facial features were undeniable. A hidden part of me was in fact disappointed in her, but in truth, this mystique made her ever more fascinating, brown eyes or green. However I had to move quickly, but Oh, so carefully.

Driving back, I checked in to the police station to see if Rob had, by some miracle, managed to extract some useful information out of our suspect. Unsurprisingly no, but was still trying. Alan was still on the paper trail of the mysterious Mr. Martin Lake, who could be, I now realised an alias for Mrs Marion Lane, using the same initial letters.

It was also extremely possible that it was Marion, in the teenage disguise of Martin Lake that had narrowly escaped our clutches earlier today. The callousness of her disregard for Alan's presence indicated a determined and desperate character. It was impossible for me tell Alan over the open telephone line, but I was going to need help.

I told him to leave what he was doing, and meet me at the industrial estate outside of town, and not to tell anyone where he was going, if asked, he was to make up an excuse.

I had decided to begin checking on Mrs Lane by starting at her place of work. Alan arrived, and I told him that Rob had given me a message for Marion and I wanted Alan to pass it on. He looked at me even more strangely when I asked him to try and check on her relationships at work, but off he went.

It was my turn to be surprised when he returned within ten minutes. "Sarge, what the Hell's going on", he said obviously annoyed "Marion doesn't work here anymore she resigned three months ago, to work for another company surely Rob knows that", he sat back clearly expecting an answer,

"I don't know whether he does", I replied hazily, for I was surprised at this turn of events. "Do they know where she went, which company she now works for", I turned on him suddenly, a thought flashed into my head.

"No, not officially, but someone saw her receive a fax with a different company name ", he hesitated. "She doesn't seem to have been the most popular of people working there, no -one was sorry to see her go", he said pulling his notebook out his inside pocket, and reading the name "EmmCee International Marketing, it's a new company on the other trading estate, you know down by the railway station".

I did know, and those phonetic initials, M.C. could they stand for Marion Crawley.

"Alan, no more questions now, just follow me and switch off your mobile phone", I did not want anyone contacting him or the other way around.

We travelled in convoy to the address Alan had been given. It was a small starter unit on the estate, and most of them had anonymous names similar to, "EmmCee International Marketing". Who knows what goes on behind these doors, I mused to myself. In my young days Industrial Estates were just that, Industrial, there was noise, and smells, and people in overalls, nowadays some of these estates are silent, ghostly even, there is no clue as to what industry, if any, actually happens on them.

The door of the unit was locked, there was no one at home, and due to the emphasis on security on estates like this, there was no way of breaking in.

"Sarge, are you going to tell me, what's happening or not", Alan asked understandably. I did under the strictest of confidences, I also told him of my need to enter this building. He nodded seriously, and asked if he could make a telephone call, I agreed as long as it was not to a police colleague, he shook his head to indicate that it was not, he was going to call in a favour.

Twenty minutes later " Mr. Keys Mobile Locksmith", turned up. Alan spoke to Mr. Keys, pointed to me and they walked to the door. The man hesitated at the lock, he wanted assurance that there would not be any repercussions on him for opening this door the assurance was swift in coming. Mr. Keys was good at his job, we were inside the unit within three minutes, we told him to wait outside, the perspiration was making the palms of my hands moist.

Inside consisted of an office, and a large work space behind a roller shutter door. The office hardware was a telephone, a fax machine, a table and chairs and a metal cupboard that was locked. In the working area, were three cars, one hidden under a large sheet. Alan snatched the sheet away and there was the small hatchback that had nearly caused his demise. He was too good an officer to touch the vehicle with his bare hands, using the sheet he tried the door handle, it too was locked, as were the other vehicles.

Mr. Keys opened cupboard and cars in an instant and retreated. All the cars were empty, but the cupboard contained a range of tracksuits, caps and trainers. I sat down in the office and breathed out a long sigh, and let my shoulders drop. I felt that at last I had broken through, and the pieces were beginning to come together depressing me by the picture they were depicting.

However, I knew I was for the first time, half a step in front. The discovery of the name, and of the factory unit obviously the operational centre, passed the initiative to me. How to use it constructively and conclusively was the immediate and increasingly pressing problem.

Alan, who was now totally aware of the situation, and equally as troubled as myself, sat across the table. I had decided on a course of

action, and he was pivotal in it. We agreed that protecting Rob was crucial if the plans were successful the subsequent results could be catastrophic to him. We would do all that we could for him, but the apprehension of a criminal, particularly where robbery and murder were concerned, had to come first.

My intention was to attempt to force Marion to act. Feed her with just enough information, to make her think discovery was imminent. Whereupon she would, I reasoned, either attempt an escape through the factory unit, changing her identity and using one of the cars, or try to obliterate her tracks by removing everything. Either way I would be waiting. She could not possibly know yet that I had uncovered her bunker, but I could not depend on that for any length of time. I had to act now. I began by disabling the cars. Cars without plug leads don't start, simple but effective.

Alan on my instructions, raced back to the station. He was to tell Rob to release our suspect, but he was also to make sure that the boy would overhear the reasons why I wanted to let him go. They were that we had bigger fish to fry. We had found the hideout at the block of flats, that address and Annie's house were being watched, but most importantly that I had uncovered the identity of " Creepy" from the school and was running that down.

Rob was also to remain at the station and wait for my call. I had to keep him out of the way just now, if he caught wind of what was happening, his emotions would make him unpredictable. Alan was to organise someone to secretly follow the boy, so that we could snatch him back when required.

I was now depending on the lad finding his options limited. No car, little money and with nowhere to stay, but with vital information. Contacting Marion immediately to pass on his knowledge and to receive instructions would be crucial for him. Alan was to go to

Marion's address post haste, watch and keep me informed of any movement. I had in the meantime, on the pretext of a drug search, procured the services of four uniformed policemen and their cars to secure the factory site. Now the question was, would she swallow the bait.

My mobile rang. It was Alan to say that the officer following the boy had reported that the boy stopped at the first public telephone box he came to, and had a lengthy conversation with someone. He was now waiting outside the box, obviously waiting for a return call, or to be picked up. He, the officer, had a car waiting to follow, should it be the latter.

So far, so good, the boy had played his part to order, but no movement from Alan's situation. Three Hours later, things still remained static. It was getting dark the street lamps were on, the workers on the estate had gone home, I wished that I could go too. My nerves were in shreds from doing nothing but waiting.

I decided to wait no longer. I rang Alan to tell him that we were to reverse positions, to wait until he saw my car, and then he could come to the unit. I decided to force the issue. Tighten the screw a little more, face to face with the enigmatic Marion.

She opened the door to my knock in T shirt and jeans, her eyes back to their natural dark brown, and hair loosely tied back, she still looked stunning.

"Oh, hi Dave, is Rob with you", she asked a little too casually I felt, but used the question to look past me, and check if there was anyone with me at all.

"Hello Marion," I responded just as casually, I wanted to be invited in, "No Rob's still at the station, checking some facts, and trying to

cope with the paperwork, he'll be home soon,"

I was trying to keep my voice at the matter of fact level, "I wondered if I could have a word with you", I asked, she smiled beautifully, stood aside and invited me in, and in the act of closing the front door I saw her check the outside once more.

"Dave, I don't want to seem rude, but I was just on my way to my aerobics class, and so haven't a great deal of time," she spoke over her shoulder as I followed her into the kitchen, as if to re-enforce her statement, she placed a sports bag on the worktop. I looked at the bag and hoped that I had not interrupted my own plan. Was she about to run, it was too late to worry about that. I was here now.

"I won't keep you ," I said, leaning nonchalantly against the antique pine kitchen units, "But, I was wondering if you had ever attended St. Agnes's Girls Grammar School", I let the question hang in the air, for a moment or two, "Only, I was out there checking on Annie Mcgovern's background from some details we found, and looking at some photographs of past students there was someone who looked just like you I thought, quite a bit younger of course", I smiled

"Who is Annie Mcgovern", she enquired from under heavily lidded eyes.

"You know", I said pointedly, but lightened it with "She was the murder victim in our present case, and we are linking her death in with all the robberies, Rob must have mentioned it,

"She looked thoughtful, "Oh yes, I do remember something now, but Rob and I haven't seen a great deal of each other lately, due obviously to this case, and I have been extremely busy at work".

I opened my mouth to mention her work, but thought better of it and kept up with "Yes, we feel Annie recognised this person, and was killed because of it".

"Really," she said picking up a apple from the fruit bowl on the table, "What brought you to that conclusion," she asked.

"Just something she wrote on the wall before she bled to death", I said with feeling, "Were you", I returned to my question.

"Were I what" she attempted a joke the air was becoming a little heavy for it.

Where you at the school", I persisted. She had moved to the cutlery draw, taken out a small knife, and began to peel the apple, carefully, as if trying to take off the peel in one, long, unbroken spiral.

"I went to several schools", she offered "We moved about as a family when I was young, due to my fathers' business ventures, St. Agnes may have been one I went to for a while". She was becoming slightly withdrawn it was as if the apple had become the centre of her attention. I decided on one more little push, and then I would leave.

"The point being, that the girl in the photograph at St. Agnes's, turns out to have had a nickname, caused by her desperate need to be the centre of attraction at all times, insecurity obviously." She was silent now and had finished peeling the apple. "The girls at the school called her Creepy, after a Creepy Crawley, you know the sort of thing. Crawley was her surname you see, no-one seems to have had a good word for her," I continued.

She was completely still now.

"Anyway, I just wondered whether you might have come across her".

I had finished and wondered had I gone too far.

She raised her head. Her face twisted with hate, and looked directly at me. Her eyes were now as black as coal. She was breathing heavily, fighting her self-control. She lost. Screaming something indecipherable, she threw the apple at me I instinctively ducked and turned my head away.

She was at me in a flash, I was off balance. She was kicking, punching and stabbing me with the paring knife. Fit, strong for her size, and now totally out of control she was everywhere.

I was trying to fend off the thrusts with my arms, whilst trying to get away but she was getting through. My hands were sticky and wet with my own blood. Backing away, something hit my head and everything swam before my eyes. I went down. Before I lost consciousness I heard a voice shouting "Marion stop", was it mine?

I came around lying on the kitchen floor. A small pool of blood emanating from the dozen or more stab wounds to my arms and upper body. I now realised how Annie McGovern had died, Marion was completely schizoid. My head still swam. I staggered to my feet and looked at my watch. I had been unconscious for twenty minutes, I had to warn Alan.

I grabbed the wall telephone in the kitchen, and rang Alan's mobile phone. "Alan", I said groggily when he answered, "She's gone, be ready, and be careful, she is really dangerous. Somehow I think the boy might be with her. I am coming and I will call for more help, its too late for secrecy now.

"Alan's voice sounded his concern, "O.K. Dave, but are you all right, you don't sound too good".

"I'll be all right, just make sure you get her Alan any way you can, don't let her get away". I leaned back against the wall. I felt grim but I had to move. I turned on the cold water tap and washed my hands and face at the kitchen sink.

Using towels and whatever I could find. I staunched the blood from the deeper cuts, and went to my car.

It was a nightmare drive. I was really a danger to myself and to others on the road. I drove like a man possessed which I suppose I was. I knew that she would go to the factory unit, and I had to be there to bring this case to a close, but could I make it in time, before I passed out, and crashed this car. Vehicles flashed by, horns blaring, as I narrowly missed them. Tyres squealed as I took bends at crazy speeds, the street lights seemed like one continuous amber line.

Somehow I arrived at the entrance to the estate there was a police car across the road as a road block. I mounted the kerb and passed it a policeman gave chase on foot. Turning into the area that held the unit there was an explosion of flashing lights, yellow, red, blue and white, the cavalry had certainly arrived. I stood on the brakes, the car screeched to a halt, and slewed half around, throwing open the door. I virtually fell out on to the cobbled roadway.

I staggered forward. Alan saw me and ran to support me before I fell, he shouted to some uniformed men to get their first aid kits out of the cars, and for someone to call an ambulance.

"Alan what has happened, where is she", I gasped, someone gave me a drink of water.

"I was ready Dave. They drove into the unit to change cars just like you thought, and whilst they were trying to get one started I drove up and blocked the entrance, trapping them inside. I had already placed men at the back, and so they are all inside the building. The only problem is that they have closed the roller shutter door and barricaded the other doors. They can't come out but we can't get in at the moment", he was pointing at the building.

Something he said registered "What do you mean all of them, there's only Marion and the boy surely," I snapped.

"I was just about to tell you Dave, Rob Lane is in there with them",

I looked at Alan, not comprehending what he meant.

"You mean she has him as a hostage", my voice rose with my temperature.

"No, he is one of them, he drove the car here", Alan's head shook as he said it "It nearly threw me, when I saw him driving, I didn't know what was happening, but it soon became clear he was not their prisoner, and so I stuck to your orders".

My mind was reeling, but I had no time to dwell on it, a voice shouted the boy's coming out and sure enough the front door opened, and the boy came running. He was yelling something I could not hear. He came nearer, and was caught in the arms of two or three policemen,.

"Get back. Get back. They are going to burn it. They have petrol from the tanks of the cars. They are not coming out".

The words had hardly left his mouth, when there was a muffled boom, and flames licked through, and under the now convex roller shutter door, and they could be seen dancing on the inside of the windows. Paint peeled in the heat. The Fire Brigade was sent for, but it was too late for those inside, as they had intended. I had made it to see the end of the case, but not as I had imagined it to be.

I was in hospital for two days, stitches, blood transfusions, and all the rest but I was all right. The indispensable Alan came several times and we discussed the events.

When I returned to work we tied up the loose ends, with information from the now very talkative Michael McGovern, Annie's son. He had been recruited by Marion, who had been looking for someone like him, in the games machine arcade in town a very likely place to find a young man with time on his hands. She had told him that he could earn plenty of money with some excitement, and little chance of discovery, taking money from people who had too much anyway.

There was something about her that frightened, and yet attracted him, I could certainly understand that. She had seemed to know all the right moves, and everything went well until that night when Annie appeared. He had not even seen her, he was putting the stolen goods in the car when Marion had appeared covered in blood, screaming at him, to get in the car. He did and they drove away.

He never read newspapers, and did not know anything was wrong, until the night he tried to go back to his house. He contacted some of his friends in the street and they told him of the murder, and who it was. He cared little for his mother, but realised the seriousness of the crime and wanted to leave. Marion had said, she would kill him too if he tried to go, and he had believed her.

She was like two people in one body, one nice and one completely

nuts. He did not even know about Rob until he picked him up from outside the telephone box. They had arrived at Rob's house, come in the back way and heard me talking to Marion. It had been Rob who had hit me, and stopped Marion from finishing me off, and they left for the factory unit to escape. They had been completely thrown when Alan and the Police had arrived. Marion was determined not to give up, she was screaming that she was never going to go to prison, and poverty, she would rather die first.

It was Marion that had collected the petrol, and Rob that at first refused, turned to let the boy out. Marion had felled him with a hammer from the boot of one of the cars, but the boy had escaped, the rest we knew.

We discovered that Rob had worked, perversely, in the Crime Prevention Unit for a while and picked some expertise in modern alarm systems, and how to install them. It was but a short step to dismantling them. He had also, as part of his duties in the unit visited many large homes and businesses, giving them advice on how to prevent theft, and so knew the potential and actual layout of many of the buildings they had robbed.

But it had been Marion, with her insatiable appetite for money, luxury and ultimately as she saw it security, born from the instability of her fathers' business ventures in her youth that had been the instigator and driving force behind the activities. Rob I believe actually loved her enough to close his eyes to the consequences. She had used the business trips abroad to set up ready-made sales for the items that they stole, and I was sure preparing for bigger things, with the new company, and the industrial unit.

It was really very sad that two young people with their lives before them, could not wait. They wanted all the material things now, they had not realised that sometimes the beauty of life together is in the chase for these acquisitions and in the strength of your love for one another in the achievement of these goals.

ABOUT THE AUTHOR

Stuart Kear was born in Ton Pentre in 1945 educated at Pentre Grammar School. He married and moved to Tonypandy where he still lives. He has three children and two grand- children. Recently his beloved wife of 47years of marriage, and to whom this collection is dedicated, passed away.

Until retirement he ran a Dry Cleaning and Laundry business in Tonypandy for ten years.

Always a lover of books and language other interests are photography, walking, quizzes, snooker and writing. He is a member of the writing group at Tonypandy Library.

A valley boy born and bred.

Printed in Great Britain
by Amazon